# Shakespeare on the Double!™

# A Midsummer Night's Dream

# Shakespeare on the Double!™

# A Midsummer Night's Dream

*translated by*

**Mary Ellen Snodgrass**

WILEY

Wiley Publishing, Inc.

*Library of Congress Cataloging-in-Publication Data:*
Shakespeare, William, 1564-1616.
  A midsummer night's dream / translated by Mary Ellen Snodgrass.
    p. cm. -- (Shakespeare on the double!)
  Original text with parallel modern English translation.
  ISBN-13: 978-0-470-21272-1 (pbk.)
  ISBN-10: 0-470-21272-1 (pbk.)
  1. Courtship--Drama. 2. Athens (Greece)--Drama. 3. Fairy plays. I. Snodgrass, Mary Ellen.
II. Title.
  PR2827.A1 2008
  822.3'3--dc22
                        2008002494
Printed in the United States of America
10  9  8  7  6  5  4  3  2  1
Book design by Melissa Auciello-Brogan
Book production by Wiley Publishing, Inc. Composition Services

# Contents

# About the Translator

**Mary Ellen Snodgrass** is an award-winning author of textbooks and general reference works, and a former columnist for the *Charlotte Observer*. A member of Phi Beta Kappa, she graduated magna cum laude from the University of North Carolina at Greensboro and Appalachian State University, and holds degrees in English, Latin, psychology, and the education of gifted children.

## ACKNOWLEDGMENT

Thanks to Dr. Suzanne Kramer Jeffers of Lenoir-Rhyne College for her advice on interpretation.

# Introduction

*S*hakespeare on the Double! *A Midsummer Night's Dream* provides the full text of the Bard's play side by side with an easy-to-read modern English translation that you can understand. You no longer have to wonder what exactly "Lord, what fools these mortals be" means! You can read the Shakespearean text on the left-hand pages and check the right-hand pages when Shakespeare's language stumps you. Or you can read only the translation, which enables you to understand the action and characters without struggling through the Shakespearean English. You can even read both, referring back and forth easily between the original text and the modern translation. Any way you choose, you can now fully understand every line of the Bard's masterpiece!

We've also provided you with some additional resources:

- **Brief synopsis** of the plot and action offers a broad-strokes overview of the play.
- **Comprehensive character list** covers the actions, motivations, and characteristics of each major player.
- **Visual character map** displays who the major characters are and how they relate to one another.
- **Cycle of love** pinpoints the sequence of love in the play, including who *truly* loves whom and who *mistakenly* loves whom.
- **Reflective questions** help you delve even more into the themes and meanings of the play.

Reading Shakespeare can be slow and difficult. No more! With *Shakespeare on the Double! A Midsummer Night's Dream,* you can read the play in language that you can grasp quickly and thoroughly.

# Synopsis

## ACT I

### Scene 1

At the palace of Duke Theseus of Athens, the famed Greek warrior anticipates marrying Hippolyta, former queen of the Amazons. In four days, the
nuptials coincide with a new moon and amusements for Athenian youth
arranged by Philostrate, master of revels. Theseus won Hippolyta in battle and plans to compensate her with a joyous ceremony. Hippolyta
assures him that time will pass quickly before their wedding day.

Egeus and his short brunette daughter Hermia arrive at court with two
rivals, Lysander and Demetrius. Egeus demands that Hermia marry
Demetrius, the man of his choice. Hermia prefers Lysander. Egeus accuses
Lysander of bewitching his daughter with original verse and love charms.
The father believes that Lysander encourages Hermia's disobedience.

Duke Theseus likes the choice of Demetrius as a suitor. The Duke
declares that, according to law, a daughter must obey her father. Hermia
learns that the punishment for disobedience is either execution or a lonely
life in a convent. Lysander declares that he is equal in status to his rival.
Unlike Demetrius, who has courted the tall blonde Helena, Lysander is
loyal to Hermia alone and not to her inheritance.

Duke Theseus intends to scold Demetrius for courting Helena and abandoning her. The Duke speaks privately to Demetrius and Egeus and warns
Hermia to obey her father. The wrangling over Hermia depresses Hippolyta.
Theseus promises to get back to discussing the entertainment at the forth-
coming wedding.

In private, Lysander reminds Hermia that love is always filled with
obstacles and unsolicited advice from friends. He proposes eluding
Athenian law by eloping 16 miles from Athens to live with his wealthy
aunt, a childless widow who adores him like a son. Outside of Athenian
jurisdiction, Hermia can escape a sentence of death or life in a convent
and can wed the man of her choice. She accepts Lysander's plan and
promises to meet him on May Day morning two and a half miles from
Athens.

Helena encounters the couple. She contrasts her looks to Hermia's
darkness. Helena marvels at Hermia's ability to charm Demetrius, even

2

though Hermia dislikes him. Hermia and Lysander divulge their plot to elope the next night and to reunite in the woods at midnight. Helena decides to inform Demetrius, whom she hopes to win away from Hermia. When Demetrius follows the couple to the woods, Helena intends to pursue him and regain her former sweetheart.

## Scene 2

Peter Quince, the carpenter, directs a band of volunteer actors whom Theseus has invited to perform a court play following the royal wedding. The players choose the tragic story of Pyramus and Thisby, two young lovers who die because of a misunderstanding. Quince assigns parts to his fellow Athenian laborers.

Nick Bottom, the weaver, accepts the starring role of Pyramus, but claims he is best at villains' parts. He wants to play all of the characters. Francis Flute, the bellows repairman, takes the role of the heroine Thisby. He is not happy to portray a female character because he wants to let his beard grow. He learns that he can wear a mask for the performance so he won't need to shave. Robin Starveling plays Thisby's mother. Tom Snout, the tin repairman, plays Pyramus's father; Quince plays Thisby's mother. Snug, the furniture maker, takes the role of the lion, which has no spoken lines.

To prove he should be the lion, Bottom claims he can roar and terrify ladies in the audience. The players worry that if the lion is too scary, it will frighten the women to death and the Duke might have the entire company hanged. Bottom agrees to moderate his roar. Quince flatters Bottom by insisting that Snug must keep the part of the lion because only Bottom can play the leading role of Pyramus. When the casting is complete, Quince sends the players off to learn their lines and tells them to meet for a rehearsal the following evening at the Duke's oak.

# ACT II

## Scene 1

The woods outside of Athens is the residence of Oberon, King of the Fairies, and of Titania, Queen of the Fairies and her company. Oberon's mischievous elf Puck, also called Robin Goodfellow, wants to keep Titania away from the woods because Oberon is approaching. Puck fears that the warring couple will meet and quarrel. Oberon is angry with Titania because she refuses to give him a sweet servant boy whom she received from the king of India. Oberon wants to add the spoiled Indian child to the forest patrol. Titania's attendant fairy accuses Puck of being the hobgoblin who annoys villagers with tricks. Puck admits that he wanders the night to harass peasants.

Oberon and Titania meet and renew their bickering. Each accuses the other of disloyalty—Oberon with Phillida and Titania with Theseus. Titania claims that Oberon's persecution of her has caused rivers to flood, grain to rot in the fields, cattle to die, frost to kill roses, and people to suffer arthritis. Oberon blames Titania for perpetuating disorder by refusing to relinquish the Indian boy. Titania keeps the boy because his mother was a dear companion and priestess who died in childbirth. Titania intends to foster the child. Ignoring Oberon's demands, the queen departs to dance with the fairies.

To win the fight, Oberon sends Puck to find a pansy blossom called love-in-idleness, which Cupid turned purple and endowed with magic by unintentionally shooting it with his arrow. When the juice of this magical flower anoints sleepers' eyelids, it creates infatuation with the first creature they see upon awakening. Oberon plans to apply the juice to Titania's eyes to make her insanely passionate for a wild beast until she relents and gives him the Indian boy.

After Puck leaves to find the purple pansy blossom, Oberon sits scheming. Demetrius and Helena stumble into his bower, but Oberon is invisible to them. Like a spaniel, Helena actively pursues Demetrius, who threatens to hurt her if she doesn't stop stalking him. After the humans depart, Puck returns with the purple pansy. Out of pity for Helena, Oberon orders his elf to anoint the eyes of the Athenian man so that he will fall in love with Helena. Puck promises to fulfill Oberon's order and departs in search of a partially identified Athenian male.

## Scene 2

On a flowery bank, Titania dances with the fairies, then sends them on errands. As she prepares for sleep, they sing her a soothing lullaby dispelling spiders and beetles. While she rests, one fairy stands guard. Oberon creeps up. He squeezes the potion onto her eyelids and casts a spell to make her arise when some vile creature comes near.

When Oberon leaves, Lysander and Hermia wander near Titania, who is invisible to them. Lysander suggests they stop for the night and find their way at daylight. Hermia agrees but won't endanger her reputation by letting him sleep beside her. After they fall asleep, Puck enters in search of an Athenian man to anoint with the magic juice. Seeing a likely candidate and Hermia lying separately, Puck applies the juice to Lysander's eyes.

After Puck exits, Helena pursues Demetrius to the bower. He sprints into the woods, leaving her to survive alone in the wild. Depressed and exhausted, Helena stops to rest and notices Lysander asleep on the ground. After she wakes him to determine whether he is alive, he instantly falls in love with her. When he claims to give up Hermia, Helena assumes he is teasing her. She runs away. Lysander leaves Hermia sleeping and chases Helena. Hermia awakens from a nightmare about a heart-eating snake and fears for Lysander's safety. She rushes into the woods.

# ACT III

## Scene 1

On a green lawn, Peter Quince and the players rehearse "Pyramus and Thisby." Bottom fears that Pyramus's suicide and the lion's roars will terrify the women in the audience. The other players agree, wondering whether they should abandon the play. Bottom proposes the addition of a prologue, explaining that Pyramus is only an actor. Bottom also suggests that Snug, the actor playing the lion, must show half of his face and must identify himself to the audience. Quince mentions their need for moonlight and a wall. After consulting a calendar and almanac, the workmen discover that the moon will be shining on the night of the performance, so they can leave a window open to natural light. Bottom proposes that an actor covered in plaster play the role of the wall. Everyone agrees, and the rehearsal begins.

Puck eavesdrops on the performance, which amuses him for its amateurish acting. While Bottom awaits his cue, Puck covers his head with an ass's head. When Bottom appears half man, half donkey, the terrified actors dash into the woods. Unaware of his transformation, Bottom has no idea what has frightened them. Puck compounds the confusion by appearing in a number of shapes and voices. As Bottom walks singing through the woods, Titania arises from sleep and claims Bottom as her love. She appoints Peaseblossom, Cobweb, Moth, and Mustardseed as Bottom's servants.

## Scene 2

Puck reports to Oberon the effects of the potion on eyelids. Oberon is pleased that Titania is enamored of Bottom and that Puck has also redirected the disdainful Athenian male toward Helena. Just after Puck assures Oberon that Demetrius loves Helena, Demetrius and Hermia enter. Puck realizes that he has bewitched the wrong Athenian. Because

Lysander has mysteriously disappeared, Hermia accuses Demetrius of murdering him and hiding the body. Demetrius insists that he didn't kill his rival, but Hermia refuses to believe him. Exhausted by the confusion, Demetrius sinks to the ground and falls asleep. Hermia continues searching for Lysander.

Oberon reprimands Puck for anointing the wrong Athenian with the magic pansy juice. Puck blames fate for the error. Oberon dispatches Puck to find Helena and anoints Demetrius's eyelids with the powerful juice. Lysander and Helena enter, still squabbling. To Puck's amusement, they awaken Demetrius, who falls in love with Helena at first sight. Hearing his declarations of love, Helena believes that Lysander and Demetrius are mocking her. When Hermia enters, Helena accuses her old friend of being part of the plot to ridicule Helena.

Hermia is shocked when Lysander declares he no longer cares for her. Helena wonders how Hermia, her closest childhood friend, could be so cruel. Helena accuses Hermia of being short and vicious; Demetrius defends Hermia from Helena's taunts. Helena runs away. Lysander and Demetrius hunt for a place to duel over possession of Helena.

Before dawn, Oberon forces Puck to fix the problem before the men attack each other. Oberon advises Puck to create a fog in which the lovers will get lost and collapse in exhaustion. When they awake in the morning, the night's events will seem like a dream and Demetrius will love Helena, his former girlfriend. Puck imitates Lysander and Demetrius's voices in the fog to befuddle them. The four rivals sink from weariness and sleep until daybreak. Oberon rushes to Titania to beg for the Indian boy.

# ACT IV

## Scene 1

Bottom enjoys Titania's bower, where she decks him with roses. Peaseblossom scratches his furry head, and Cobweb searches for a snack of honey. Bottom orders oats and hay for a meal. As he sleeps in Titania's arms, Oberon pities his wife for loving an ass. To soothe Oberon, Titania sends a fairy to transfer the servant boy to Oberon's quarters. Oberon squeezes an antidote from the chaste tree on her eyes to release her from the spell. Titania awakens, telling Oberon about her strange dream of being in love with an ass. Oberon has Puck remove the ass's head from Bottom. Before the lark announces dawn, the king and queen of fairies dance and awaken the Athenian couples. The royal fairies hurry off to bless Hippolyta and Theseus's union.

During a celebration of May Day, Theseus, Hippolyta, and Egeus walk through the woods at daybreak with hunters and baying hounds. When Theseus spies the sleeping lovers, Egeus identifies them, but wonders why rivals like Demetrius and Lysander sleep near each other. Theseus concludes that they exhausted themselves in early morning from observing the rite of May. Theseus declares it the day that Hermia must choose her future, death or a convent. When the dazed lovers arise, Demetrius explains why he followed Lysander and Hermia on their elopement. Demetrius rejects Hermia and claims Helena for his sweetheart.

Theseus sets the lovers' double wedding at the time of his and Hippolyta's nuptials. As the foursome returns to the palace with the Duke and Hippolyta, Bottom awakens and tries to understand what has happened to him. He proposes having Peter Quince write a ballad about the confusing events. The weaver names the poem "Bottom's Dream" because it has no bottom. He intends to sing the ballad after Thisby dies.

## Scene 2

At Quince's house in Athens, he and Flute search for Bottom, who has not yet returned home. They fear that they can't perform "Pyramus and Thisby" without the male lead. The actors believe that Theseus will reward Bottom with a lifelong pension of six cents a day for his performance. As they lament the weaver's lost opportunity, Bottom suddenly returns. His friends want to hear his story, but Bottom tells them there isn't time because the Duke has finished the wedding dinner. Before the play, Bottom warns the actors to put on clean costumes, to secure masks and pumps, and to avoid onions and garlic so their breath will be sweet.

# ACT V

## Scene 1

After the three newly married couples leave the temple, Quince and his players arrive at the palace. Theseus and Hippolyta discuss the strange tale the lovers have told them. When the joyous couples enter, Theseus considers a list of proposed festivities for the evening. After ruling out two weighty poems and a satire that Philostrate proposes, the Duke chooses "Pyramus and Thisby." Theseus is intrigued by the paradoxes in the play, which is both merry and tragic, tedious and brief. Philostrate tries to dissuade Theseus from sitting through the silly scenario, but Theseus thinks the simple fare by dutiful Athenians deserves a hearing.

The players present "Pyramus and Thisby," accompanied by the viewers' critical asides. Hippolyta is disgusted by the poor quality of acting, but Theseus is touched by the loyalty of local workers. He argues that even the best actors create only a brief illusion. True enjoyment of drama requires the audience's imagination. Following the performance, Bottom asks Theseus whether he'd like to hear an epilogue or watch an Italian peasant dance from Bergamo. Theseus opts for the dance, having lost patience with the players' ineptness.

At midnight, the gathering breaks up. Puck sweeps the stage while commenting on drama. Oberon and Titania arrive with a procession of fairies. The company blesses the house and the newlyweds' future children. Puck apologizes for the weakness of the performance and promises that the next production will be better.

# List of Characters

**THESEUS**   The proud Duke of Athens and a cousin of the mythic strongman Hercules, Theseus is a mature lover who eagerly anticipates marriage to Hippolyta, an Amazon queen he captured in battle. He listens to the noble Egeus's complaint about his disobedient daughter Hermia and renders judgment on a child's duties to a parent. Although sympathizing with Hermia, he upholds an anti-female law denying women control of their future. He counsels Hermia with his personal philosophy that marriage makes women blossom. Midway through the play, Duke Theseus displays a host's graciousness by leading Hippolyta on a May Day hunt and arranging a triple wedding ceremony. He prefers reason over fables and fairy tales, a fastidiousness suited to a military man. Nonetheless, he honors the lower-class mechanicals, even when their flowery compliments are nonsensical and their theatrical performance a sham.

**HIPPOLYTA**   The former Queen of the Amazons, Hippolyta is the captured bride of the warlike Theseus. Because of her circumstances at the court of Athens, she pities Hermia the choice between execution and confinement to a convent as punishment for refusing an arranged marriage to Demetrius. Refined and ladylike, Hippolyta soothes Theseus's ardor in the four days remaining before their wedding. Unlike her captor, she enjoys imaginative tales and commiserates with the lovers' difficult Midsummer Night in the woods. At the post-wedding performance of "Pyramus and Thisby," she exhibits a judgmental side of her character by mocking the ineptness of Robin Starveling, the clumsy actor who plays Moonshine. By the play's end, she admits to feeling sympathy for Pyramus, who grieves his love's violent death.

**OBERON**   The king of the fairies, Oberon stands out from other characters for his selfishness and overbearing personality. He is given to eavesdropping and assumes the right to torment his wife, Queen Titania, and to steal her Indian boy servant. Oberon's plotting causes havoc on earth from wet wintry weather that bedevils humankind. After hastily dispatching his agent Puck to intervene in lovers' quarrels, Oberon gentles his spirit, pities his wife's humiliating infatuation with an ass-headed weaver, and orders a restoration of lovers to their original mates. In the resolution, Oberon honors marriage for siring children.

9

**TITANIA**   The beloved mistress of the fairies, Queen Titania enjoys nightly frolics with her energetic sprites, who shield her from harm. During a separation from her quarrelsome husband Oberon, she accuses him of flirtation with Phillida and infatuation with Hippolyta. Titania's humanity shames Oberon for the misery he causes farmers and herders. In maternal fashion, Titania treasures the Indian boy servant, whose mother, Titania's priestess and confidante, died in childbirth. During Titania's bewitching, she generously bestows jewels and servants to sing Bottom to sleep. She nestles him while he rests and strokes his long ears, a motherly act devoid of lust. After the triple wedding, she displays her benevolence in blessing the palace.

**PUCK**   The overconfident fairy trickster named Robin Goodfellow, Puck is a "knavish sprite" who arranges mischief at the command of King Oberon. Puck breaches standards of courtesy and exults in sadistic mayhem that befuddles humans and violates the order of the seasons. He studies the king's moods and wards off domestic fights between Oberon and Titania to keep his master jovial and amused. Puck's indifference to human suffering suggests a goblin run amuck. Although he is a court servant, he disdains the acting troupe as ignorant yokels and dismisses mortals as simpletons. At the end of his prank on the four lovers, he leaves Demetrius besotted with Helena. In contrast to Puck's original character, he sweeps the stage at play's end and apologizes to any playgoer who might be offended by the production.

**EGEUS**   An old-fashioned Athenian father, Egeus insists on the right of the male parent to determine his daughter's future. Disgruntled at court, he attempts to sway Duke Theseus to execute Lysander for wooing Hermia. At play's end, Egeus is the only character who fails to grow in humanity and compassion. He finds the ruler less vengeful than himself and more sympathetic to Hermia's plight for rejecting Demetrius.

**HERMIA**   A short, dark-skinned brunette with a fiery temper, Hermia exhibits the defiance of fatherly control that set Renaissance women against outdated laws and traditions of the Middle Ages. At one time, she shared with Helena a sisterhood that bound them in singing and embroidery. Hermia's maturity is evident in her willingness to vacate her father's house and to follow Lysander by abandoning her homeland and marrying outside of Athenian jurisdiction. On the way to Lysander's aunt's house, Hermia graciously leaves the field clear for Helena to win Demetrius. After Puck's interference bungles the pairing of Hermia with Lysander and Helena with Demetrius, Hermia takes on a militant pose and defends her love for a worthy man.

**HELENA**    A willowy blonde noblewoman and daughter of Nedar, Helena envies the dark Mediterranean beauty of her old friend Hermia and abases herself with exaggerated claims of ugliness. In stalking Demetrius, an uncommitted male who betrayed her, Helena exhibits the faults of a love-stricken maiden willing to grovel to an abusive male. At a plot twist that has two men courting her, Helena is bewildered and pathetically vulnerable. Overwhelmed by a double pursuit, she fears smug ridicule from the two men rather than sincere courtship. Out of sorts with being the butt of humor, she belittles her old friend Hermia as dark, dwarfish, and scheming and claims to run faster.

**DEMETRIUS**    A noble suitor of Hermia, Demetrius has a reputation for disloyalty. Unlike the loving Lysander, Demetrius wants to possess Hermia like a prize, even if he must commit violence against his rival. He gains the affections of Egeus, but not of his daughter, who prefers Lysander. To Helena, who gushes her infatuation for Demetrius, he is curt, dismissive, and menacing in his reference to rape in an isolated wood and in threatening Helena with peril. After Puck releases the lovers from a magic spell, Demetrius settles into the role of contented bridegroom and enjoys ridiculing the acting troupe.

**LYSANDER**    A witty, self-assured young nobleman, Lysander claims himself the equal of his rival Demetrius in wealth and heritage and implies that he is the better man. Lysander cleverly courts Hermia with standard Elizabethan love gifts, a serenade, flowers, and original verse. At a face-off at Duke Theseus's court, Lysander cheerily invites Demetrius to wed Egeus rather than Hermia. It is Lysander's elopement plan that sets in motion the mix-up in the forest on Midsummer Night, the eve of the summer solstice on June 25. On the long walk to his aunt's house, he displays concern for Hermia's weariness and respects her modesty by sleeping apart from her. He is scrappy enough to challenge Demetrius to a duel.

**PETER QUINCE**    A carpenter among the Athenian "mechanicals," Peter Quince is a laborer who proposes entertaining the Duke on his wedding night with an original production of the Greek myth "Pyramus and Thisby," which he writes and stages. Peter's methods are orderly and his directions clear. He is farsighted enough to realize that frightening the Duchess and her ladies could result in death sentences for the acting troupe. He also foresees a need for private rehearsals to conceal the group's art. He tactfully keeps the over-eager Nick Bottom in line and leads a search for his star after Bottom disappears. At the postnuptial performance, Peter demonstrates limited literal skills when he misreads the prologue.

**NICK BOTTOM**    A self-important weaver among the Athenian "mechanicals," Nick bears a clownish name suggesting Shakespeare's focus on low comic relief from a potentially serious dramatic situation resulting in a girl's execution. He intrudes on the direction of Peter Quince, who obeys Bottom's orders. Playing Pyramus, Bottom belabors the troupe with opinions and anticipates earning a pension of sixpence a day for his performance. After Puck transforms him with an ass's head, he finds himself wooed by the gorgeous queen of the fairies. Without realizing he is the victim of a prank, he sinks into luxury as though it were his right. Unruffled by his release from a magic spell, he performs his stage role with appropriate absurdity.

**SNUG**    A joiner, or furniture maker, Snug aids five other "mechanicals" in performing "Pyramus and Thisby." Less conceited than Nick Bottom, Snug admits to being slow at learning a role. To reassure the audience, he explains that he only pretends to be a lion.

**TOM SNOUT**    The timorous tin repairer among the Athenian "mechanicals," Tom Snout acts the part of the wall that separates the title lovers in "Pyramus and Thisby." He makes himself ridiculous by holding his fingers in a vee to represent a chink in the wall.

**ROBIN STARVELING**    An Athenian tailor, Robin Starveling joins the five "mechanicals" by playing Moonshine. Following the folk traditions of the Man in the Moon, he carries a lantern and thorn bush and leads a dog. His appearance draws heckling from the audience.

**FRANCIS FLUTE**    An apprenticed Athenian adolescent, Flute studies bellows mending. Although he flaunts the beginnings of a manly beard, his name implies that his voice has not changed. He is squeamish about the acts of lovers and sees himself in the idealized role of a wandering knight. At Peter's insistence, Flute grudgingly agrees to play the female role of Thisby by holding a mask over his face and speaking in a womanish voice.

**PHILOSTRATE**    The master of the revels at Duke Theseus's court, Philostrate exhibits order and judgment against a backdrop of muddles. At the wedding of Hippolyta and Theseus, Philostrate assumes a pompous air in rejecting the five artisans' amateurish play, which brought him to tears from laughing at the rehearsal. Like the uppity Puck, Philostrate snubs ignorant laborers.

**PEASEBLOSSOM**    A gentle fairy, Peaseblossom is one of four attendants to Queen Titania during her infatuation with the ass-headed Nick Bottom. Peaseblossom obliges Bottom by scratching his itchy donkey's head, a duty shared with the fairy **MUSTARDSEED**.

**COBWEB**   A third attendant fairy, Cobweb locates honey for Bottom. The name cobweb causes Bottom to refer to the folk use of spider webs as a coagulant for bleeding.

**MOTH**   The fourth fairy attendant on Bottom, Moth is a mere wisp in the romantic scenario between the long-eared lover and Queen Titania.

# Character Map

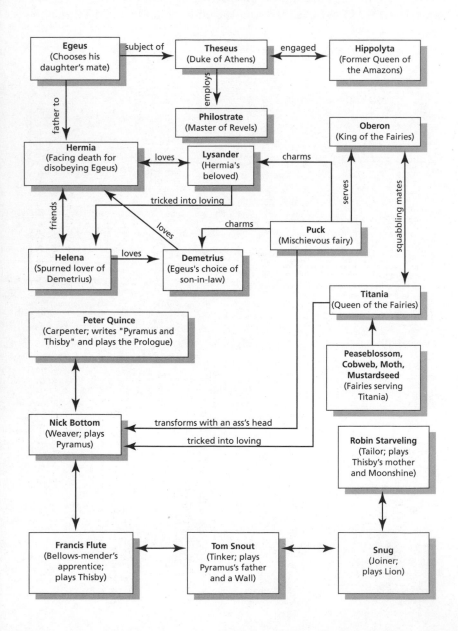

# Cycle of Love

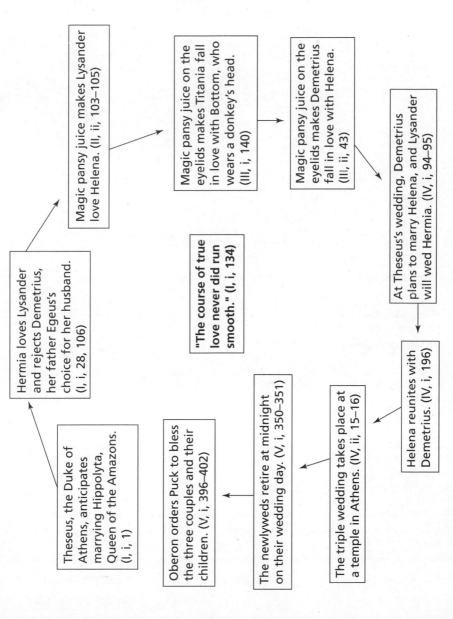

Hermia loves Lysander and rejects Demetrius, her father Egeus's choice for her husband. (I, i, 28, 106)

Magic pansy juice makes Lysander love Helena. (II, ii, 103–105)

Magic pansy juice on the eyelids makes Titania fall in love with Bottom, who wears a donkey's head. (III, i, 140)

Magic pansy juice on the eyelids makes Demetrius fall in love with Helena. (III, ii, 43)

At Theseus's wedding, Demetrius plans to marry Helena, and Lysander will wed Hermia. (IV, i, 94–95)

"The course of true love never did run smooth." (I, i, 134)

Theseus, the Duke of Athens, anticipates marrying Hippolyta, Queen of the Amazons. (I, i, 1)

Oberon orders Puck to bless the three couples and their children. (V, i, 396–402)

The newlyweds retire at midnight on their wedding day. (V, i, 350–351)

The triple wedding takes place at a temple in Athens. (IV, ii, 15–16)

Helena reunites with Demetrius. (IV, 196)

# Shakespeare's
# A Midsummer Night's Dream

# ACT I, SCENE 1

Athens, and a nearby wood.

*[Enter THESEUS, HIPPOLYTA, PHILOSTRATE, with others]*

THESEUS          Now, fair Hippolyta, our nuptial hour
                 Draws on apace; four happy days bring in
                 Another moon; but, o, methinks, how slow
                 This old moon wanes! She lingers my desires,
                 Like to a step-dame or a dowager,                    5
                 Long withering out a young man's revenue.

HIPPOLYTA        Four days will quickly steep themselves in night;
                 Four nights will quickly dream away the time;
                 And then the moon, like to a silver bow
                 New bent in heaven, shall behold the night           10
                 Of our solemnities.

THESEUS                              Go, Philostrate,
                 Stir up the Athenian youth to merriments;
                 Awake the pert and nimble spirit of mirth;
                 Turn melancholy forth to funerals;
                 The pale companion is not for our pomp.              15
                 *[Exit PHILOSTRATE]*
                 Hippolyta, I wooed thee with my sword,
                 And won thy love doing thee injuries;
                 But I will wed thee in another key,
                 With pomp, with triumph, and with revelling.
                 *[Enter EGEUS and his daughter HERMIA, and LYSANDER, and*
                 *DEMETRIUS]*

EGEUS            Happy be Theseus, our renowned Duke!                 20

THESEUS          Thanks, good Egeus. What's the news with thee?

# ACT I, SCENE 1

The Greek city-state of Athens and a nearby forest.

*[THESEUS, Duke of Athens, enters with HIPPOLYTA, Queen of the Amazons, PHILOSTRATE, master of court entertainment, and others.]*

THESEUS — Our wedding is only four days away, beautiful Hippolyta. It coincides with a new moon. The time passes so slowly. The moon delays my fulfillment of love like a stepmother or widow spending a young man's inheritance.

HIPPOLYTA — Four days will quickly slip by. Four nights will bring you pleasant dreams. Then the new moon, like a bow aiming an arrow in the sky, will shine on our wedding ceremony.

THESEUS — Philostrate, offer amusements to the young people of Athens. Encourage their perky, agile love of fun. Leave sadness for burials. Our ceremony should not be a time for grieving. *[PHILOSTRATE leaves on his assignment.]* Hippolyta, I captured you by sword and courted you roughly. But our wedding will be glorious, triumphant, and joyous. *[EGEUS enters with his daughter HERMIA and HERMIA'S two suitors, LYSANDER and DEMETRIUS.]*

EGEUS — I wish you gladness, Duke Theseus.

THESEUS — Thank you, Egeus. How are you?

| EGEUS | Full of vexation come I, with complaint |
|---|---|
| | Against my child, my daughter Hermia. |
| | Stand forth, Demetrius!—My noble lord, |
| | This man hath my consent to marry her. | 25 |
| | Stand forth, Lysander!—And, my gracious Duke, |
| | This man hath bewitched the bosom of my child. |
| | Thou, thou, Lysander, thou hast given her rhymes, |
| | And interchanged love-tokens with my child. |
| | Thou hast by moonlight at her window sung | 30 |
| | With feigning voice verses of feigning love, |
| | And stolen the impression of her fantasy |
| | With bracelets of thy hair, rings, gauds, conceits, |
| | Knacks, trifles, nosegays, sweetmeats—messengers |
| | Of strong prevailment in unhardened youth; | 35 |
| | With cunning hast thou filched my daughter's heart; |
| | Turned her obedience, which is due to me, |
| | To stubborn harshness. And, my gracious Duke, |
| | Be it so she will not here before your grace |
| | Consent to marry with Demetrius, | 40 |
| | I beg the ancient privilege of Athens; |
| | As she is mine I may dispose of her; |
| | Which shall be either to this gentleman |
| | Or to her death, according to our law |
| | Immediately provided in that case. | 45 |

EGEUS
: Full of vexation come I, with complaint
Against my child, my daughter Hermia.
Stand forth, Demetrius!—My noble lord,
This man hath my consent to marry her. 25
Stand forth, Lysander!—And, my gracious Duke,
This man hath bewitched the bosom of my child.
Thou, thou, Lysander, thou hast given her rhymes,
And interchanged love-tokens with my child.
Thou hast by moonlight at her window sung 30
With feigning voice verses of feigning love,
And stolen the impression of her fantasy
With bracelets of thy hair, rings, gauds, conceits,
Knacks, trifles, nosegays, sweetmeats—messengers
Of strong prevailment in unhardened youth; 35
With cunning hast thou filched my daughter's heart;
Turned her obedience, which is due to me,
To stubborn harshness. And, my gracious Duke,
Be it so she will not here before your grace
Consent to marry with Demetrius, 40
I beg the ancient privilege of Athens;
As she is mine I may dispose of her;
Which shall be either to this gentleman
Or to her death, according to our law
Immediately provided in that case. 45

THESEUS
: What say you, Hermia? Be advised, fair maid.
To you your father should be as a god,
One that composed your beauties; yea, and one
To whom you are but as a form in wax,
By him imprinted, and within his power 50
To leave the figure, or disfigure it.
Demetrius is a worthy gentleman.

HERMIA
: So is Lysander.

THESEUS
: In himself he is;
But, in this kind, wanting your father's voice,
The other must be held the worthier. 55

HERMIA
: I would my father looked but with my eyes.

THESEUS
: Rather your eyes must with his judgment look.

**EGEUS** I am annoyed with my daughter Hermia, who tries my patience. Stand here, Demetrius! Theseus, I have chosen this man to marry Hermia. Stand here, Lysander! This man has won my daughter's affections. Lysander, you have written her poems and exchanged love gifts with her. You have sung love songs outside her window in moonlight. You have crept into her heart with bracelets woven from your hair, baubles, gimmicks, knickknacks, toys, little bouquets, and sweet treats—all powerful enticements to an inexperienced girl. You have stolen Hermia's heart by trickery. You have transformed her obedience to me into waywardness. Duke Theseus, if she stands before you and refuses to wed Demetrius, I seek the father's legal privilege to rid myself of her. She must either marry Demetrius or be killed immediately, according to Athenian law.

**THESEUS** What is your answer, Hermia? I warn you, young girl. You should reverence Egeus like a god for siring a beautiful daughter. Because he gave you life, he has the power to let you live or to destroy you. Demetrius is a worthy choice for a husband.

**HERMIA** Lysander is also a worthy choice for a mate.

**THESEUS** You're right—he's a likely suitor. But Demetrius is the better man because your father chose him for you.

**HERMIA** I wish my father would look at Lysander as I do.

**THESEUS** You must look at Demetrius with Egeus's wisdom.

| HERMIA | I do entreat your grace to pardon me. |
|---|---|
| | I know not by what power I am made bold, |
| | Nor how it may concern my modesty | 60 |
| | In such a presence here to plead my thoughts: |
| | But I beseech your grace that I may know |
| | The worst that may befall me in this case |
| | If I refuse to wed Demetrius. |

**HERMIA**

I do entreat your grace to pardon me.
I know not by what power I am made bold,
Nor how it may concern my modesty                    60
In such a presence here to plead my thoughts:
But I beseech your grace that I may know
The worst that may befall me in this case
If I refuse to wed Demetrius.

**THESEUS**

Either to die the death, or to abjure                65
For ever the society of men.
Therefore, fair Hermia, question your desires,
Know of your youth, examine well your blood,
Whether, if you yield not to your father's choice,
You can endure the livery of a nun;                  70
For aye to be in shady cloister mewed,
To live a barren sister all your life,
Chanting faint hymns to the cold, fruitless moon.
Thrice-blessed they that master so their blood
To undergo such maiden pilgrimage:                   75
But earthlier happy is the rose distilled
Than that which, withering on the virgin thorn,
Grows, lives, and dies, in single blessedness.

**HERMIA**

So will I grow, so live, so die, my lord,
Ere I will yield my virgin patent up                 80
Unto his lordship, whose unwished yoke
My soul consents not to give sovereignty.

**THESEUS**

Take time to pause; and by the next new moon,
The sealing-day betwixt my love and me
For everlasting bond of fellowship,                  85
Upon that day either prepare to die
For disobedience to your father's will,
Or else to wed Demetrius, as he would;
Or on Diana's altar to protest
For aye austerity and single life.                   90

**DEMETRIUS**

Relent, sweet Hermia; and, Lysander, yield
Thy crazed title to my certain right.

**LYSANDER**

You have her father's love, Demetrius;
Let me have Hermia's—do you marry him.

**EGEUS**

Scornful Lysander, true, he hath my love;            95
And what is mine my love shall render him;
And she is mine; and all my right of her
I do estate unto Demetrius.

| | |
|---|---|
| **HERMIA** | Excuse me, Duke Theseus. I don't know why I am so pushy. I may violate modesty by pleading my case to a duke. Tell me the worst fate that awaits me if I disobey my father and refuse to marry Demetrius. |
| **THESEUS** | You will either be executed or give up all men. Therefore, young Hermia, search your heart. Examine your spirit and youth and decide whether you are willing to withdraw to a convent as punishment for disobeying Egeus. For the rest of your life, you will remain a virgin imprisoned in a nunnery singing hymns to chastity. Nuns earn three blessings for remaining virgins. But women are happier by living an earthly life that blossoms normally. |
| **HERMIA** | I choose to grow up, live, and die a nun rather than obey my father. I refuse to give my love to the man he chooses for my husband. |
| **THESEUS** | Think over your decision. By the new moon four days from now, I will wed Hippolyta. On that day, you will accept the death penalty for disobeying Egeus or you will marry Demetrius as Egeus commands. Your only other choice is servitude to Diana, the goddess of chastity, who demands a stark single life. |
| **DEMETRIUS** | Say yes, Hermia. Lysander, give up your claim on her to me, the rightful suitor. |
| **LYSANDER** | Egeus loves you, Demetrius. Let me marry Hermia and you marry Egeus. |
| **EGEUS** | Lysander, you make a joke of my preference for Demetrius as a son-in-law. I offer affection to him by betrothing Hermia to him. She is mine. I give her and my wealth to Demetrius. |

TRANSLATION

LYSANDER I am, my lord, as well derived as he,
As well possessed; my love is more than his; 100
My fortunes every way as fairly ranked,
If not with vantage, as Demetrius';
And, which is more than all these boasts can be,
I am beloved of beauteous Hermia:
Why should not I then prosecute my right? 105
Demetrius, I'll avouch it to his head,
Made love to Nedar's daughter, Helena,
And won her soul; and she, sweet lady, dotes,
Devoutly dotes, dotes in idolatry,
Upon this spotted and inconstant man. 110

THESEUS I must confess that I have heard so much,
And with Demetrius thought to have spoke thereof;
But, being over-full of self-affairs,
My mind did lose it. But, Demetrius, come;
And come, Egeus; you shall go with me; 115
I have some private schooling for you both.
For you, fair Hermia, look you arm yourself
To fit your fancies to your father's will,
Or else the law of Athens yields you up—
Which by no means we may extenuate— 120
To death, or to a vow of single life.
Come, my Hippolyta: what cheer, my love?
Demetrius, and Egeus, go along;
I must employ you in some business
Against our nuptial, and confer with you 125
Of something nearly that concerns yourselves.

EGEUS With duty and desire we follow you.
*[Exeunt all but LYSANDER and HERMIA]*

LYSANDER How now, my love? Why is your cheek so pale?
How chance the roses there do fade so fast?

HERMIA Belike for want of rain, which I could well 130
Beteem them from the tempest of my eyes.

LYSANDER Ay me! for aught that I could ever read,
Could ever hear by tale or history,
The course of true love never did run smooth:
But either it was different in blood— 135

HERMIA O cross!—too high to be enthralled to low!

LYSANDER Or else misgraffed in respect of years—

HERMIA O spite!—too old to be engaged to young!

ORIGINAL

| LYSANDER | I have noble heritage and wealth. I love Hermia more than he does. My future is even more promising than that of Demetrius. And, more important, Hermia loves me. Why shouldn't I demand my right to her? I say to Demetrius's face that he courted Helena, Nedar's daughter, and won her love. Helena idolizes this fickle, disloyal man. |
|---|---|
| THESEUS | I confess that I have heard of Demetrius's wooing of Helena. I intended to scold Demetrius about his faithlessness. But I have been so busy that I forgot. Demetrius and Egeus, go with me. I want to speak privately to you both. Hermia, transfer your love to Demetrius, as Egeus demands. Or else, you must obey Athenian law, which I must enforce. Choose either execution or the life of a nun. Hippolyta, dear, have we depressed you? Demetrius and Egeus, precede me. I need your help with my wedding plans. And I want to discuss your own problems. |
| EGEUS | We follow you as dutiful, eager Athenians. *[When the others depart, LYSANDER and HERMIA remain.]* |
| LYSANDER | Are you well, Hermia? Why are you so pale? What happened to your rosy cheeks? |
| HERMIA | My roses need rain, which I can supply with tears. |
| LYSANDER | Oh, me. According to all I have read in fiction and history, true love was never easy. Either the lovers were of different social classes— |
| HERMIA | A misfortune for too high a person to love too low a person! |
| LYSANDER | Or else the pair is mismatched in age— |
| HERMIA | A hardship when too old a person seeks a young lover! |

TRANSLATION

| LYSANDER | Or else it stood upon the choice of friends— |

| HERMIA | O hell, to choose love by another's eyes! | 140 |

LYSANDER    Or, if there were a sympathy in choice,
War, death, or sickness, did lay siege to it,
Making it momentany as a sound,
Swift as a shadow, short as any dream,
Brief as the lightning in the collied night          145
That, in a spleen, unfolds both heaven and earth,
And ere a man hath power to say, 'Behold!'
The jaws of darkness do devour it up.
So quick bright things come to confusion.

HERMIA      If then true lovers have been ever crossed,      150
It stands as an edict in destiny.
Then let us teach our trial patience,
Because it is a customary cross,
As due to love as thoughts, and dreams, and sighs,
Wishes and tears, poor fancy's followers.          155

LYSANDER    A good persuasion. Therefore, hear me, Hermia.
I have a widow aunt, a dowager
Of great revenue, and she hath no child.
From Athens is her house remote seven leagues;
And she respects me as her only son.          160
There, gentle Hermia, may I marry thee;
And to that place the sharp Athenian law
Cannot pursue us. If thou lov'st me then,
Steal forth thy father's house tomorrow night,
And in the wood, a league without the town,          165
Where I did meet thee once with Helena
To do observance to a morn of May,
There will I stay for thee.

HERMIA                    My good Lysander!
I swear to thee by Cupid's strongest bow,
By his best arrow with the golden head,          170
By the simplicity of Venus' doves,
By that which knitteth souls and prospers loves,
And by that fire which burned the Carthage queen,
When the false Trojan under sail was seen,
By all the vows that ever men have broke—          175
In number more than ever women spoke—
In that same place thou hast appointed me,
Tomorrow truly will I meet with thee.

ORIGINAL

**LYSANDER**  Or the match depends on friends' advice—

**HERMIA**  A torment to let someone else select the perfect mate!

**LYSANDER**  Or, if the match turned out favorably, illness, death, or combat destroyed it, making it as short-lived as a sound, swift as a shadow, brief as a dream, or as quick as lightning on a black night. In a burst of wrath, the sky and land appear. Before the viewer can comment on the display, the dark sky swallows the flash. That's how rapidly a bright vision vanishes.

**HERMIA**  If fate has always parted lovers, destiny must demand their separation. Let's live with this obstacle. Because parting is a standard problem for lovers, it is as natural an occurrence as loving thoughts, dreams, sighs, wishes, and fears—the fruits of imagination.

**LYSANDER**  Good advice. Hermia, I have a wealthy aunt who is childless. She lives over 16 miles from Athens. She treats me like an only son. I can marry you at her house, Hermia. Because she lives away from Athens, we will avoid local law. If you are still willing, sneak out of Egeus's house tomorrow night. I will wait for you in the woods around two and a half miles from Athens, in the spot where I encountered you and Helena celebrating a May morning.

**HERMIA**  My dear Lysander, I swear to you by the strongest bow of Cupid, the god of infatuation. By his arrow with the gold arrowhead. By the gentleness of the doves of Venus, the goddess of passion. By whatever joins souls and furthers romance. By the funeral pyre that devoured Dido, Queen of Carthage, when the Trojan hero Aeneas abandoned her. By every vow that males have broken. More numerous than the vows that women pledged, I will meet you tomorrow in the place you named.

| | |
|---|---|
| LYSANDER | Keep promise, love. Look, here comes Helena.<br>*[Enter HELENA]* |
| HERMIA | God speed, fair Helena! Whither away?   180 |
| HELENA | Call you me fair? That fair again unsay.<br>Demetrius loves your fair—O happy fair!<br>Your eyes are lodestars, and your tongue's sweet air<br>More tuneable than lark to shepherd's ear,<br>When wheat is green, when hawthorn buds appear.   185<br>Sickness is catching. O, were favour so,<br>Yours would I catch, fair Hermia, ere I go;<br>My ear should catch your voice, my eye your eye,<br>My tongue should catch your tongue's sweet melody.<br>Were the world mine, Demetrius being bated,   190<br>The rest I'd give to be to you translated.<br>O, teach me how you look, and with what art<br>You sway the motion of Demetrius' heart! |
| HERMIA | I frown upon him, yet he loves me still. |
| HELENA | O that your frowns would teach my smiles such skill!   195 |
| HERMIA | I give him curses, yet he gives me love. |
| HELENA | O that my prayers could such affection move! |
| HERMIA | The more I hate, the more he follows me. |
| HELENA | The more I love, the more he hateth me. |
| HERMIA | His folly, Helena, is no fault of mine.   200 |
| HELENA | None but your beauty; would that fault were mine! |
| HERMIA | Take comfort: he no more shall see my face;<br>Lysander and myself will fly this place.<br>Before the time I did Lysander see,<br>Seemed Athens as a paradise to me:   205<br>O, then, what graces in my love do dwell,<br>That he hath turned a heaven unto hell! |
| LYSANDER | Helen, to you our minds we will unfold:<br>To-morrow night, when Phoebe doth behold<br>Her silver visage in the watery glass,   210<br>Decking with liquid pearl the bladed grass,<br>A time that lovers' flights doth still conceal,<br>Through Athens' gates have we devised to steal. |

ORIGINAL

| | |
|---|---|
| LYSANDER | Keep your word, dear. Look, here comes Helena.<br>*[HERMIA's friend HELENA enters.]* |
| HERMIA | Greetings, fair Helena! Where are you going? |
| HELENA | Do you think I'm fair? Take back your words. Demetrius loves your good looks. Lucky you! Your eyes are guiding stars to him. Your words seem more melodious than the lark to a shepherd in spring, when wheat turns green and buds appear on the hawthorn tree. Some illness is contagious. I would love to catch your infection, Hermia, before I leave. I want your voice, your eyes, and the sound of your words. Except for Demetrius, I would give you my whole world. Show me how to copy your looks and the way that you win Demetrius's love! |
| HERMIA | I refuse him, but he still loves me. |
| HELENA | I would like to turn my smiles into your frowns! |
| HERMIA | I curse him, but he continues to love me. |
| HELENA | I wish that my prayers could win his affection! |
| HERMIA | The more I hate him, the more he pursues me. |
| HELENA | The more I adore him, the more he hates me. |
| HERMIA | Helena, his foolishness is not my fault. |
| HELENA | Nothing but your looks, which I wish I had! |
| HERMIA | Don't worry. I shall disappear from his sight. Lysander and I will elope. Before I met Lysander, I loved Athens like a paradise. My fondness for Lysander has turned Athens into a punishment. |
| LYSANDER | Helena, we will tell you our plan. Tomorrow night, when water reflects the image of the moon and turns the dewdrops on blades of grass into pearls, at a time when lovers sneak away, we plan to slip through the gates of Athens. |

ACT 1

TRANSLATION

HERMIA
    And in the wood where often you and I
    Upon faint primrose beds were wont to lie,    215
    Emptying our bosoms of their counsel sweet,
    There my Lysander and myself shall meet:
    And thence from Athens turn away our eyes,
    To seek new friends and stranger companies.
    Farewell, sweet playfellow. Pray thou for us,    220
    And good luck grant thee thy Demetrius!
    Keep word, Lysander. We must starve our sight
    From lovers' food, till morrow deep midnight.

LYSANDER
    I will, my Hermia.
    *[Exit HERMIA]*

LYSANDER
              Helena, adieu:
    As you on him, Demetrius dote on you!    225
    *[Exit LYSANDER]*

HELENA
    How happy some o'er other some can be!
    Through Athens I am thought as fair as she.
    But what of that? Demetrius thinks not so;
    He will not know what all but he do know.
    And as he errs, doting on Hermia's eyes,    230
    So I, admiring of his qualities.
    Things base and vile, holding no quantity,
    Love can transpose to form and dignity.
    Love looks not with the eyes, but with the mind;
    And therefore is winged Cupid painted blind.    235
    Nor hath love's mind of any judgment taste;
    Wings and no eyes figure unheedy haste:
    And therefore is love said to be a child,
    Because in choice he is so oft beguiled.
    As waggish boys in game themselves forswear,    240
    So the boy Love is perjured everywhere.
    For ere Demetrius looked on Hermia's eyne,
    He hailed down oaths that he was only mine;
    And when this hail some heat from Hermia felt,
    So he dissolved, and showers of oaths did melt.    245
    I will go tell him of fair Hermia's flight;
    Then to the wood will he to-morrow night
    Pursue her; and for this intelligence
    If I have thanks, it is a dear expense;
    But herein mean I to enrich my pain,    250
    To have his sight thither and back again.
    *[Exit]*

ACT I

| | |
|---|---|
| HERMIA | To the woods where you and I rested on beds of primroses, telling each other our secrets, Lysander and I plan to meet. We will move away from Athens to live among strangers and new friends. Goodbye, old pal. Pray for our success and may good fortune give you Demetrius! Keep your promise, Lysander. We must remain apart until midnight tomorrow. |
| LYSANDER | I will keep my promise, Hermia. *[HERMIA departs.]* |
| LYSANDER | God be with you, Helena. I hope that Demetrius soon adores you as much as you worship him! *[LYSANDER departs.]* |
| HELENA | Some people seem so much happier than others! Athenians think I am just as pretty as Hermia. It doesn't matter what they think if Demetrius doesn't agree with them. He doesn't want to know that I am pretty. So, he fails to find love in Hermia and I fail to win his affection. Love can transform worthless, wretched things into worthy shapes. Love is a mental emotion, not a visual treat. That is why artists paint Cupid as blind. Love lacks judgment. Like Cupid, love flies rapidly and blindly away. Love is like a child because it is easily tricked. Just as boys lie during silly games, so does Love tell lies. Before Demetrius gazed at Hermia, he bombarded me with pledges to be true to me. His love for me, like hailstones melted by love for Hermia, turned his vows to water. I will inform him of Hermia's elopement. He will follow her to the woods tomorrow night. If he thanks me, I will be surprised. But telling Hermia's secret is my way of winning back Demetrius's love. *[HELENA goes out.]* |

# ACT I, SCENE 2

## Another part of Athens.

*[Enter QUINCE the Carpenter, and SNUG the Joiner, and BOTTOM the Weaver, and FLUTE the Bellows-mender, and SNOUT the Tinker, and STARVELING the Tailor]*

| | |
|---|---|
| QUINCE | Is all our company here? |
| BOTTOM | You were best to call them generally, man by man, according to the scrip. |
| QUINCE | Here is the scroll of every man's name which is thought fit through all Athens to play in our interlude before the Duke and the Duchess on his wedding-day at night. |
| BOTTOM | First, good Peter Quince, say what the play treats on; then read the names of the actors; and so grow to a point. |
| QUINCE | Marry, our play is 'The most lamentable comedy and most cruel death of Pyramus and Thisby'. |
| BOTTOM | A very good piece of work, I assure you, and a merry. Now, good Peter Quince, call forth your actors by the scroll. Masters, spread yourselves. |
| QUINCE | Answer as I call you. Nick Bottom, the weaver? |
| BOTTOM | Ready. Name what part I am for, and proceed. |
| QUINCE | You, Nick Bottom, are set down for Pyramus. |
| BOTTOM | What is Pyramus? A lover or a tyrant? |
| QUINCE | A lover that kills himself most gallantly for love. |

5

10

15

20

# ACT I, SCENE 2

In another section of Athens.

*[Some workers—QUINCE the carpenter, SNUG the furniture maker, BOTTOM the weaver, FLUTE the bellows mender, SNOUT the tin repairman, and STARVELING the tailor—arrive together.]*

| | |
|---|---|
| QUINCE | Has everyone arrived? |
| BOTTOM | You should call the roll, laborer by laborer. |
| QUINCE | Here is a list of every Athenian chosen to perform a short play on the wedding night of Duke Theseus and Queen Hippolyta. |
| BOTTOM | Peter Quince, describe the action of the play, name the actors, and get to the point. |
| QUINCE | The play is entitled "The sad comedy and cruel deaths of Pyramus and Thisby." |
| BOTTOM | A well-written drama, I promise, and funny. Peter, call the roll of actors. Workers, spread out. |
| QUINCE | Answer to your name. Nick Bottom, the weaver? |
| BOTTOM | Here. What part do I play? |
| QUINCE | You, Nick, play Pyramus. |
| BOTTOM | Who is Pyramus, a lover or a villain? |
| QUINCE | He is a lover who commits suicide for love. |

TRANSLATION

| | |
|---|---|
| **BOTTOM** | That will ask some tears in the true performing of it. If I do it, let the audience look to their eyes: I will move storms; I will condole in some measure. To the rest—yet my chief humour is for a tyrant: I could play Ercles rarely, or a part to tear a cat in, to make all split: |

'The raging rocks
And shivering shocks
Shall break the locks
Of prison gates,
And Phibbus' car
Shall shine from far,
And make and mar
The foolish Fates.'

25

30

This was lofty. Now name the rest of the players. 35
This is Ercles' vein, a tyrant's vein; a lover
is more condoling.

**QUINCE**    Francis Flute, the bellows-mender?

**FLUTE**    Here, Peter Quince.

**QUINCE**    Flute, you must take Thisby on you.    40

**FLUTE**    What is Thisby? A wandering knight?

**QUINCE**    It is the lady that Pyramus must love.

**FLUTE**    Nay, faith, let not me play a woman; I have a
beard coming.

**QUINCE**    That's all one; you shall play it in a mask, and    45
you may speak as small as you will.

**BOTTOM**    An I may hide my face, let me play Thisby too.
I'll speak in a monstrous little voice; 'Thisne,
Thisne!'—'Ah, Pyramus, my lover dear; thy
Thisby dear! and lady dear!'    50

**QUINCE**    No, no, you must play Pyramus; and, Flute,
you Thisby.

**BOTTOM**    Well, proceed.

**QUINCE**    Robin Starveling, the tailor?

**STARVELING**    Here, Peter Quince.    55

| | |
|---|---|
| BOTTOM | I will have to weep during my performance. If I weep, the audience will weep. I will raise storms of sadness. Then I will comfort the weepers. Get on with the rest of the actors. But I am best at playing a villain. I would play a unique version of Hercules. I could do well at ranting and raising an uproar. |
| | The angry rocks and the quivering cornstalks will burst locks on prison doors. The sun god's chariot will gleam at a distance and will overwhelm destiny. |
| | That was a grand speech. List the other actors. I just spoke like Hercules, the villain. I must be more consoling to be a lover. |
| QUINCE | Francis Flute, the bellows mender? |
| FLUTE | Present, Peter Quince. |
| QUINCE | Flute, you will play Thisby. |
| FLUTE | Who is Thisby? A traveling horseman? |
| QUINCE | Thisby is Pyramus's lover. |
| FLUTE | No, please, I don't want to play a woman's part. I am beginning to sprout a beard. |
| QUINCE | It doesn't matter. You will wear a mask and speak in a tiny voice. |
| BOTTOM | If I can hide my face with a mask, let me have the part of Thisby, too. I can mimic a tiny voice. 'Thisne, Thisne!' 'Pyramus, my dear love, I am your dear lady Thisby!' |
| QUINCE | No, Bottom, you must play Pyramus, and Flute, you play Thisby. |
| BOTTOM | Okay. Keep assigning parts. |
| QUINCE | Robin Starveling, the tailor? |
| STARVELING | Present, Peter Quince. |

TRANSLATION

| | |
|---|---|
| QUINCE | Robin Starveling, you must play Thisby's<br>mother. Tom Snout, the tinker? |
| SNOUT | Here, Peter Quince. |
| QUINCE | You, Pyramus' father; myself, Thisby's father;<br>Snug, the joiner, you, the lion's part; and, I hope,<br>here is a play fitted. |
| SNUG | Have you the lion's part written? Pray you, if it<br>be, give it me, for I am slow of study. |
| QUINCE | You may do it extempore, for it is nothing but<br>roaring. |
| BOTTOM | Let me play the lion too: I will roar that I will<br>do any man's heart good to hear me; I will roar<br>that I will make the Duke say 'Let him roar again,<br>let him roar again!' |
| QUINCE | An you should do it too terribly, you<br>would fright the Duchess and the ladies, that they<br>would shriek; and that were enough to hang us<br>all. |
| ALL | That would hang us, every mother's son. |
| BOTTOM | I grant you, friends, if you should fright the<br>ladies out of their wits, they would have no more<br>discretion but to hang us; but I will aggravate<br>my voice so, that I will roar you as gently as<br>any sucking dove; I will roar you an 'twere any<br>nightingale. |
| QUINCE | You can play no part but Pyramus; for Pyramus<br>is a sweet-faced man; a proper man, as one shall<br>see in a summer's day; a most lovely gentleman-<br>like man; therefore you must needs play<br>Pyramus. |
| BOTTOM | Well, I will undertake it. What beard were I best<br>to play it in? |
| QUINCE | Why, what you will. |
| BOTTOM | I will discharge it in either your straw-colour<br>beard, your orange-tawny beard, your purple-in-<br>grain beard, or your French-crown-colour<br>beard, your perfect yellow. |

60

65

70

75

80

85

90

| | |
|---|---|
| QUINCE | Robin Starveling, you will play the part of Thisby's mother. Tom Snout, the tin repairman? |
| SNOUT | Present, Peter Quince. |
| QUINCE | You will play Pyramus's father; I will play Thisby's father. Snug, the furniture maker, you will take the lion's role. That should take care of role assignments. |
| SNUG | Do you have a copy of the lion's speeches? If you do, let me have it. I memorize slowly. |
| QUINCE | You may improvise it. You only have to roar. |
| BOTTOM | I want to be the lion, too. I will roar enough to suit any listener. I will roar so well that Duke Theseus will demand, "Make him roar again, make him roar again!" |
| QUINCE | If you roar too well, you may scare the Duchess and other ladies and make them scream. The Duke might send us to the gallows. |
| ALL | They would execute every one of us. |
| BOTTOM | If you terrorize the women, the court might have no choice but to execute us. I will throw my voice and roar as softly as a baby dove. I will roar like a nightingale. |
| QUINCE | You have to play Pyramus. Pyramus has a tender smile. He is an admirable person, like a gentleman strolling on a summer's day. You have to play Pyramus. |
| BOTTOM | Okay, I will play Pyramus. What beard should I choose? |
| QUINCE | Whatever you want. |
| BOTTOM | I will choose from straw color, a yellow-orange, a permanent purple, or the color of a gold coin, a perfect yellow. |

QUINCE      Some of your French crowns have no hair at
            all, and then you will play bare-faced. But, masters,
            here are your parts, and I am to entreat you,                    95
            request you, and desire you, to con them by to-
            morrow night; and meet me in the palace wood,
            a mile without the town, by moonlight; there
            will we rehearse: for if we meet in the city, we
            shall be dogged with company, and our devices         100
            known. In the meantime I will draw a bill of
            properties, such as our play wants. I pray you,
            fail me not.

BOTTOM      We will meet; and there we may rehearse most
            obscenely and courageously. Take pains; be              105
            perfect; adieu!

QUINCE      At the Duke's oak we meet.

BOTTOM      Enough; hold, or cut bow-strings.
            *[Exeunt]*

ORIGINAL

QUINCE      Some French heads have lost their hair to venereal dis-
            ease, so you would play without a beard. Workmen, here
            are your parts. I beg that you memorize them by tomor-
            row night. Meet me in the palace woods a mile from
            Athens by moonlight. We will rehearse there. If we prac-
            tice in Athens, people will cluster about and learn our
            stage tricks. Meanwhile, I will list the props that our play
            calls for. Please, be dependable.

BOTTOM      We will gather in the woods and rehearse courageously
            on the scene. Do your best, memorize your parts. God go
            with you!

QUINCE      We will meet next at the Duke's oak tree.

BOTTOM      Enough talking. Keep your word or we fail. *[The workers
            depart.]*

# ACT II, SCENE 1

A wood near Athens.

*[Enter a FAIRY at one door, and ROBIN GOODFELLOW at another]*

| | |
|---|---|
| PUCK | How now, spirit: whither wander you? |
| FAIRY | Over hill, over dale, |

Thorough bush, thorough brier,
Over park, over pale,
Thorough flood, thorough fire,                                              5
I do wander everywhere,
Swifter than the moon's sphere;
And I serve the fairy queen,
To dew her orbs upon the green.
The cowslips tall her pensioners be:                                       10
In their gold coats spots you see;
Those be rubies, fairy favours,
In those freckles live their savours;
I must go seek some dew-drops here,
And hang a pearl in every cowslip's ear.                                   15
Farewell, thou lob of spirits; I'll be gone.
Our queen and all her elves come here anon.

PUCK       The king doth keep his revels here to-night;
Take heed the Queen come not within his sight.
For Oberon is passing fell and wrath,                                      20
Because that she as her attendant hath
A lovely boy, stol'n from an Indian king;
She never had so sweet a changeling;
And jealous Oberon would have the child
Knight of his train, to trace the forests wild:                           25
But she perforce withholds the loved boy,
Crowns him with flowers, and makes him all her joy.
And now they never meet in grove or green,
By fountain clear, or spangled starlight sheen,
But they do square, that all their elves for fear                         30
Creep into acorn cups, and hide them there.

# ACT II, SCENE 1

Woods outside the Greek city-state of Athens.

*[A FAIRY enters from one side of the stage; ROBIN GOODFELLOW enters from the other side.]*

**PUCK**    Well, sprite, where are you going?

**FAIRY**    I go over hill and meadow, through bushes and under-brush, over park and fenced-in land, through water and fire. I travel everywhere swifter than the round moon. As the fairy queen's servant, I sprinkle dew over dance cir-cles in the grass. Yellow swamp primulas are her security guards. You can see spots on their gold jackets. The spots are ruby flower centers, sweet-smelling freckles that the fairies gave them. I must look for dew drops. I will hang one in each flower, like a pearl earring. Goodbye, you lump of the spirit world. I'm on my way. Titania, our queen, and her attendant elves are coming here soon.

**PUCK**    Oberon, the King of Fairies, is holding amusements here tonight. Be sure Oberon doesn't see Titania. Oberon is in a raging mood because Titania keeps a pretty boychild for her attendant. She stole him from a king of India. She has never owned so sweet a captured human child. Oberon is jealous and wants the boy for one of his atten-dants to patrol the woods. But Titania keeps the adored child for herself. She crowns the boy with flowers and delights in him. Now, Titania and Oberon never meet in groves or meadows; whether by clear spring or starry sky, the two quarrel. The arguments frighten the fairies so much that they hide in empty acorns.

ACT II

TRANSLATION

FAIRY

Either I mistake your shape and making quite,
Or else you are that shrewd and knavish sprite
Called Robin Goodfellow. Are not you he
That frights the maidens of the villagery,                          35
Skim milk, and sometimes labour in the quern,
And bootless make the breathless housewife churn;
And sometime make the drink to bear no barm;
Mislead night-wanderers, laughing at their harm?
Those that Hobgoblin call you, and sweet Puck,                      40
You do their work, and they shall have good luck:
Are not you he?

PUCK

          Thou speak'st aright;
I am that merry wanderer of the night.
I jest to Oberon, and make him smile,
When I a fat and bean-fed horse beguile,                            45
Neighing in likeness of a filly foal;
And sometime lurk I in a gossip's bowl,
In very likeness of a roasted crab;
And, when she drinks, against her lips I bob,
And on her withered dewlap pour the ale.                            50
The wisest aunt, telling the saddest tale,
Sometime for three-foot stool mistaketh me;
Then slip I from her bum, down topples she,
And 'tailor' cries, and falls into a cough;
And then the whole quire hold their hips and loff,                  55
And waxen in their mirth, and neeze, and swear
A merrier hour was never wasted there.
But room, fairy, here comes Oberon.

FAIRY

And here my mistress. Would that he were gone!
*[Enter OBERON, the King of the Fairies, at one door, with his
Train; and TITANIA, the Queen, at another, with hers]*

FAIRY    Either I misidentify your shape, or else you are that cunning rascal elf named Robin Goodfellow. Aren't you the mischief-maker who terrifies village girls? You skim cream from milk and grind grain in the handmill and stop the housewife from churning milk into butter. And sometimes you stop the ale from fermenting. You mislead people in the dark and laugh at their confusion. Aren't you the spirit who brings good fortune to those who call you Hobgoblin and Puck?

PUCK    You are correct. I wander merrily at night. I entertain Oberon and make him smile, by tricking a fat, overfed stallion by whinnying like a young filly. Sometimes I hide in the punch bowl of a friendly chatterer and take the shape of a roasted crabapple. When she sips, I bob up against her mouth; I dribble ale on her wrinkled double chin. The wisest old auntie, telling the most serious story, sometimes mistakes me for a three-legged stool. I slip away from her rump, letting her fall. She cries out and coughs. And then her friends grab their hips and laugh. As the merriment increases, they sneeze and declare that they have never had more fun wasting an hour. Move back, fairy, here comes Oberon, King of the Fairies.

FAIRY    And here comes Queen Titania. I wish that Oberon weren't here! *[OBERON, King of the Fairies, precedes his company through one side of the stage while QUEEN TITANIA and her retinue enter at the other side.]*

ACT II

TRANSLATION

| | | |
|---|---|---|
| **OBERON** | Ill met by moonlight, proud Titania. | 60 |
| **TITANIA** | What, jealous Oberon? Fairies, skip hence;<br>I have forsworn his bed and company. | |
| **OBERON** | Tarry, rash wanton! Am not I thy lord? | |
| **TITANIA** | Then I must be thy lady; but I know<br>When thou hast stol'n away from fairy land,<br>And in the shape of Corin sat all day,<br>Playing on pipes of corn, and versing love<br>To amorous Phillida. Why art thou here,<br>Come from the farthest steep of India,<br>But that, forsooth, the bouncing Amazon,<br>Your buskined mistress and your warrior love,<br>To Theseus must be wedded, and you come<br>To give their bed joy and prosperity? | 65<br><br><br><br><br>70 |
| **OBERON** | How canst thou thus, for shame, Titania,<br>Glance at my credit with Hippolyta,<br>Knowing I know thy love to Theseus?<br>Didst not thou lead him through the glimmering night<br>From Perigenia, whom he ravished?<br>And make him with fair Aegles break his faith,<br>With Ariadne and Antiopa? | 75<br><br><br><br>80 |

ORIGINAL

| | |
|---|---|
| **OBERON** | I'm sorry to meet you in the moonlight, uppity Titania. |
| **TITANIA** | What did you say, envious Oberon? Fairies, skip on ahead. I have abandoned Oberon. |
| **OBERON** | Stay here, bold woman! Am I not your husband? |
| **TITANIA** | Then I am your wife. But I know that you have crept out of fairy land. You have taken the shape of the shepherd Corin. All day, you play panpipes and talk of love to flirty Phillida. And why have you returned? You come from the high mountains of India. Indeed, Hippolyta, the warlike maid in boots, will marry Duke Theseus. Have you come to shower their union with happiness and fertility? |
| **OBERON** | Shame on you, Titania. How can you accuse me of loving Hippolyta when you have a crush on Theseus? Didn't you lead him through the starry night from Perigenia, the maid he raped? Didn't you make Theseus abandon Aegles to court both Ariadne and Antiopa? |

ACT II

| TITANIA | These are the forgeries of jealousy: |
| | And never, since the middle summer's spring, |
| | Met we on hill, in dale, forest, or mead, |
| | By paved fountain, or by rushy brook, |
| | Or on the beached margent of the sea, |

These are the forgeries of jealousy:
And never, since the middle summer's spring,
Met we on hill, in dale, forest, or mead,
By paved fountain, or by rushy brook,
Or on the beached margent of the sea,                    85
To dance our ringlets to the whistling wind,
But with thy brawls thou hast disturbed our sport.
Therefore the winds, piping to us in vain,
As in revenge, have sucked up from the sea
Contagious fogs; which, falling in the land,             90
Hath every pelting river made so proud
That they have overborne their continents:
The ox hath therefore stretched his yoke in vain,
The ploughman lost his sweat; and the green corn
Hath rotted ere his youth attained a beard.              95
The fold stands empty in the drowned field,
And crows are fatted with the murrion flock;
The nine men's morris is filled up with mud,
And the quaint mazes in the wanton green
For lack of tread are undistinguishable:                 100
The human mortals want their winter here;
No night is now with hymn or carol blest:
Therefore the moon, the governess of floods,
Pale in her anger, washes all the air,
That rheumatic diseases do abound:                       105
And thorough this distemperature we see
The seasons alter: hoary-headed frosts
Fall in the fresh lap of the crimson rose;
And on old Hiems' thin and icy crown
An odorous chaplet of sweet summer buds                  110
Is, as in mockery, set. The spring, the summer,
The childing autumn, angry winter, change
Their wonted liveries; and the mazed world,
By their increase, now knows not which is which:
And this same progeny of evils comes                     115
From our debate, from our dissension:
We are their parents and original.

OBERON     Do you amend it, then: it lies in you.
Why should Titania cross her Oberon?
I do but beg a little changeling boy                     120
To be my henchman.

| | |
|---|---|
| TITANIA | These are the made-up stories of a jealous man. Since springtime, you have interrupted my fairies on hill, valley, woods, and meadow, by pebbled spring and by the cattails along the brook, or on the seashore, where we dance in a circle against the wind. Because of your vengeance, unhealthful fogs swept in from the sea and kept us from dancing in the wind. Your dampness has filled rivers and made them overflow. The plowman has wasted the ox's energy in the fields. Unripe grain rotted before maturing. The sheep pen lies empty in the soggy field. Crows fatten themselves on the diseased cattle. Muck fills the outline of lawn checkers. And the imaginative paths in the grass grow over from lack of use. People have no winter. They stop singing hymns and carols. The moon, creator of floods, sheds pale light. People suffer from arthritis. The seasons shift in this unseasonable weather. Frost whitens red rosebuds. In a mockery of the seasons, a fragrant ring of summer blossoms crowns the thinning hair of aged Winter. Spring, summer, fruitful fall, and harsh winter lose their accustomed colors. And people, alarmed by the turmoil, don't know one season from another. This evil period comes from our quarrel and anger. We are the cause of upset in nature. |

ACT II

| | |
|---|---|
| OBERON | You fix it. It's your fault. Why should Titania disobey her husband? All I want is the little boy to serve as my page. |

| TITANIA | Set your heart at rest; |
|---|---|
| | The fairy land buys not the child of me. |

TITANIA                    Set your heart at rest;
The fairy land buys not the child of me.
His mother was a vot'ress of my order:
And, in the spiced Indian air, by night,
Full often hath she gossiped by my side,                    125
And sat with me on Neptune's yellow sands,
Marking th' embarked traders on the flood;
When we have laughed to see the sails conceive
And grow big-bellied with the wanton wind;
Which she, with pretty and with swimming gait             130
Following, her womb then rich with my young squire,
Would imitate, and sail upon the land,
To fetch me trifles, and return again
As from a voyage, rich with merchandise.
But she, being mortal, of that boy did die;                135
And for her sake do I rear up her boy;
And for her sake I will not part with him.

OBERON           How long within this wood intend you stay?

TITANIA          Perchance till after Theseus' wedding-day.
If you will patiently dance in our round,                  140
And see our moonlight revels, go with us.
If not, shun me, and I will spare your haunts.

OBERON           Give me that boy and I will go with thee.

TITANIA          Not for thy fairy kingdom. Fairies, away:
We shall chide downright if I longer stay.                 145
*[Exit TITANIA and her Train]*

OBERON           Well, go thy way: thou shalt not from this grove
Till I torment thee for this injury.
My gentle Puck, come hither: thou rememb'rest
Since once I sat upon a promontory,
And heard a mermaid, on a dolphin's back                   150
Uttering such dulcet and harmonious breath
That the rude sea grew civil at her song
And certain stars shot madly from their spheres
To hear the sea-maid's music.

PUCK                                    I remember.

ORIGINAL

| | |
|---|---|
| **TITANIA** | Forget it. You couldn't buy the boy from me for all of fairy land. His mother was my priestess. She often chatted with me at night in the fragrant air of India. She sat with me on the beach and watched merchant ships on the tide. We laughed at the wind filling the sails. She was pregnant with the boy. With a pretty step, she fetched me delights. She returned from errands like a heavily stocked sloop calling into port. She died in childbirth. Out of love for her, I am fostering her baby. Because of her loyalty to me, I will not give him up. |
| **OBERON** | How long will you stay in the woods? |
| **TITANIA** | Perhaps for four days, until after Theseus's wedding. If you want to dance in the fairy circles and watch our nighttime fun, you are welcome. If you won't join us, then leave me alone and I will avoid your favorite spots. |
| **OBERON** | Give me the child and I will go with you. |
| **TITANIA** | Not if you gave me your kingdom. Fairies, let's go. If I stay any longer, we will fight openly. *[TITANIA and her company depart.]* |
| **OBERON** | Well, go. You won't leave the woods until I repay you for refusing my request. Puck, come here. Do you remember when I sat on a jut of land? We listened to a mermaid as she rode a dolphin over the sea and calmed the waves by singing. Shooting stars crossed the sky to hear her melody. |
| **PUCK** | I recall. |

ACT II

OBERON      That very time I saw, but thou couldst not,           155
            Flying between the cold moon and the earth,
            Cupid, all armed: a certain aim he took
            At a fair vestal, throned by the west,
            And loosed his love-shaft smartly from his bow
            As it should pierce a hundred thousand hearts;        160
            But I might see young Cupid's fiery shaft
            Quenched in the chaste beams of the watery moon;
            And the imperial vot'ress passed on,
            In maiden meditation, fancy-free.
            Yet marked I where the bolt of Cupid fell:            165
            It fell upon a little western flower,
            Before milk-white; now purple with love's wound,
            And maidens call it 'love-in-idleness.'
            Fetch me that flower, the herb I showed thee once;
            The juice of it on sleeping eyelids laid              170
            Will make or man or woman madly dote
            Upon the next live creature that it sees.
            Fetch me this herb, and be thou here again
            Ere the leviathan can swim a league.

PUCK        I'll put a girdle round about the earth               175
            In forty minutes!
            [Exit]

OBERON                          Having once this juice,
            I'll watch Titania when she is asleep,
            And drop the liquor of it in her eyes:
            The next thing then she waking looks upon—
            Be it on lion, bear, or wolf, or bull,               180
            On meddling monkey, or on busy ape—
            She shall pursue it with the soul of love.
            And ere I take this charm from off her sight—
            As I can take it with another herb—
            I'll make her render up her page to me.               185
            But who comes here? I am invisible,
            And I will overhear their conference.
            [Enter DEMETRIUS, HELENA following him]

**OBERON**    That same night, I saw something you didn't see. I saw Cupid with his bow and arrow flying toward the moon. He aimed his arrow at a pretty maiden sitting on a throne. Cupid shot his arrow through a hundred thousand hearts. I could see the hot arrow cooled by the moon's pure rays. The priestess moved out of range of the arrow and escaped infatuation. I saw where the arrow fell. It landed on a milky white flower. The arrow turned the white flower purple. Young girls call the blossom the pansy. Bring me the purple flower that I once showed you. Pansy juice dropped on sleeping eyes will make the human crazy in love for the next person who comes into sight. Bring me the blossom before a whale can swim two and a half miles.

**PUCK**    I can fly around the globe in forty minutes! *[PUCK departs.]*

**OBERON**    When I have the pansy juice, I will wait until Titania sleeps and drop it on her eyes. The next creature she sees—whether lion, bear, wolf, bull, nosy monkey, or ape—she will fall madly in love with. Before I relieve her of this passion with an antidote, I will make her give up the boy. Who is coming? Because I am invisible, I will eavesdrop. *[DEMETRIUS enters with HELENA following him.]*

DEMETRIUS     I love thee not, therefore pursue me not.
              Where is Lysander and fair Hermia?
              The one I'll slay, the other slayeth me.                    190
              Thou told'st me they were stol'n into this wood,
              And here am I, and wood within this wood,
              Because I cannot meet with Hermia.
              Hence, get thee gone, and follow me no more.

HELENA        You draw me, you hard-hearted adamant!                      195
              But yet you draw not iron, for my heart
              Is true as steel. Leave you your power to draw,
              And I shall have no power to follow you.

DEMETRIUS     Do I entice you? Do I speak you fair?
              Or, rather, do I not in plainest truth                      200
              Tell you I do not, nor I cannot love you?

HELENA        And even for that do I love you the more.
              I am your spaniel; and, Demetrius,
              The more you beat me, I will fawn on you:
              Use me but as your spaniel, spurn me, strike me,            205
              Neglect me, lose me; only give me leave,
              Unworthy as I am, to follow you.
              What worser place can I beg in your love—
              And yet a place of high respect with me—
              Than to be used as you use your dog?                        210

DEMETRIUS     Tempt not too much the hatred of my spirit;
              For I am sick when I do look on thee.

HELENA        And I am sick when I look not on you.

DEMETRIUS     You do impeach your modesty too much,
              To leave the city, and commit yourself                      215
              Into the hands of one that loves you not;
              To trust the opportunity of night,
              And the ill counsel of a desert place,
              With the rich worth of your virginity.

HELENA        Your virtue is my privilege, for that.                      220
              It is not night when I do see your face,
              Therefore I think I am not in the night;
              Nor doth this wood lack worlds of company,
              For you, in my respect, are all the world.
              Then how can it be said I am alone                          225
              When all the world is here to look on me?

| | |
|---|---|
| **DEMETRIUS** | I don't love you, so go away. Where are Lysander and Hermia? I will kill him. She already kills me with her beauty. They told me they were eloping to the woods. I am here, enraged because I can't have Hermia. Go away, Helena, and stop following me. |
| **HELENA** | You lure me, you hard-hearted magnet! You are not pulling iron, because my heart is true like steel. Give up your power over me, and I will stop loving you. |
| **DEMETRIUS** | Have I courted you? Do I speak loving words? Haven't I told you plainly that I don't love you? |
| **HELENA** | Despite your words, I love you even more. I am your pet dog. The more you hit me, Demetrius, the more I adore you. Treat me like your favorite spaniel. Despise me, hit me, neglect me, abandon me. Let me follow you, even if I don't deserve you. What lower place can I take—but a place I respect—than to be your pet? |
| **DEMETRIUS** | Don't try my patience. I am sick of you. |
| **HELENA** | I am sick when I don't see you. |
| **DEMETRIUS** | You are immodest to leave Athens and offer yourself to a man who doesn't love you. You walk alone by night in a barren place, where someone could rape you. |
| **HELENA** | I choose to follow your good qualities. It isn't dark where I can see you. I don't see the night as dark. It isn't lonely here in the woods. With you nearby, I have all the world. How can I be walking alone with the whole world looking at me? |

ACT II

TRANSLATION

DEMETRIUS      I'll run from thee, and hide me in the brakes,
And leave thee to the mercy of wild beasts.

HELENA      The wildest hath not such a heart as you.
Run when you will, the story shall be changed;    230
Apollo flies, and Daphne holds the chase;
The dove pursues the griffin; the mild hind
Makes speed to catch the tiger—bootless speed,
When cowardice pursues and valour flies.

DEMETRIUS      I will not stay thy questions. Let me go;    235
Or, if thou follow me, do not believe
But I shall do thee mischief in the wood.

HELENA      Ay, in the temple, in the town, the field,
You do me mischief. Fie, Demetrius!
Your wrongs do set a scandal on my sex.    240
We cannot fight for love as men may do;
We should be wooed, and were not made to woo.
*[Exit DEMETRIUS]*
I'll follow thee, and make a heaven of hell,
To die upon the hand I love so well.
*[Exit]*

OBERON      Fare thee well, nymph. Ere he do leave this grove,    245
Thou shalt fly him, and he shall seek thy love.
*[Enter PUCK]*
Hast thou the flower there? Welcome, wanderer.

PUCK      Ay, there it is.

| | |
|---|---|
| **DEMETRIUS** | I'll run away and hide in the underbrush. I will leave you unguarded from wild animals. |
| **HELENA** | No wild animal can have a heart like yours. Run away and change the ancient myth. Apollo flees from Daphne. The dove chases the eagle-headed lion. The doe speeds after the tiger. You run in vain. When the coward follows you, your courage departs. |
| **DEMETRIUS** | I won't stand here and listen. Let me go. If you follow me into the woods, I will harm you. |
| **HELENA** | You harm me in the church, in Athens, in the field. Shame on you, Demetrius! Your mistreatment of me wrongs all women. Women aren't supposed to be the aggressors. Women are meant to be courted. We shouldn't chase men. *[DEMETRIUS departs.]* I will pursue you and bedevil you into loving me. I will die trying to gain the man I love. *[She departs.]* |
| **OBERON** | Goodbye, maiden. Before Demetrius leaves the woods, you will flee from him and he will pursue you. *[PUCK returns.]* Did you bring the pansy? Welcome back, traveler. |
| **PUCK** | Yes, here it is. |

ACT II

| OBERON | I pray thee give it me. |
| | I know a bank whereon the wild thyme blows, |
| | Where oxlips and the nodding violet grows; | 250 |
| | Quite over-canopied with luscious woodbine, |
| | With sweet musk-roses, and with eglantine: |
| | There sleeps Titania sometime of the night, |
| | Lulled in these flowers with dances and delight; |
| | And there the snake throws her enamelled skin, | 255 |
| | Weed wide enough to wrap a fairy in; |
| | And with the juice of this I'll streak her eyes, |
| | And make her full of hateful fantasies. |
| | Take thou some of it, and seek through this grove: |
| | A sweet Athenian lady is in love | 260 |
| | With a disdainful youth. Anoint his eyes; |
| | But do it when the next thing he espies |
| | May be the lady. Thou shalt know the man |
| | By the Athenian garments he hath on. |
| | Effect it with some care, that he may prove | 265 |
| | More fond on her than she upon her love. |
| | And look thou meet me ere the first cock crow. |
| | |
| PUCK | Fear not, my lord; your servant shall do so. |
| | *[Exeunt]* |

**OBERON**    Give it to me. I know a bank of wild thyme where prim-
roses and violets grow. Overhead grow honeysuckle,
musk-scented roses, and sweetbrier. Titania sleeps among
the blossoms at night after dancing with the fairies.
There the snake sheds its skin in a strip wide enough to
wrap a fairy in. I will dot her eyes with pansy juice and
fill her with terrible longings. You take some and search
the woods. A sweet Athenian girl loves an unloving man.
Wet his eyes with the juice. Arrange it so he will next
look on the girl. You will recognize him by his Athenian
dress. Do it carefully so he becomes fonder of her than
she of him. Meet me here before daybreak.

ACT II

**PUCK**    Don't worry, I will do my best. *[They go out.]*

TRANSLATION

# ACT II, SCENE 2

Another part of the wood.

*[Enter TITANIA, Queen of the Fairies, with her Train]*

TITANIA           Come, now a roundel and a fairy song,
                       Then, for the third part of a minute, hence:
                       Some to kill cankers in the musk-rose buds,
                       Some war with reremice for their leathern wings,
                       To make my small elves coats, and some keep back    5
                       The clamorous owl, that nightly hoots and wonders
                       At our quaint spirits. Sing me now asleep;
                       Then to your offices, and let me rest.
                       *[FAIRIES sing]*

FIRST FAIRY      *[Singing]* You spotted snakes, with double tongue,
                       Thorny hedgehogs, be not seen;    10
                       Newts and blindworms do no wrong;
                       Come not near our Fairy Queen.

CHORUS             *[Singing]* Philomel, with melody,
                       Sing in our sweet lullaby:
                       Lulla, lulla, lullaby; lulla, lulla, lullaby:    15
                       Never harm
                       Nor spell, nor charm,
                       Come our lovely lady nigh.
                       So good-night, with lullaby.

SECOND FAIRY   *[Singing]* Weaving spiders, come not here;    20
                       Hence, you long-legged spinners, hence;
                       Beetles black, approach not near;
                       Worm nor snail do no offence.

CHORUS             *[Singing]* Philomel with melody, etc.
                       *[TITANIA sleeps]*

FIRST FAIRY      Hence away; now all is well.    25
                       One, aloof, stand sentinel.
                       *[Exeunt FAIRIES; Enter OBERON; He drops the juice on
                       TITANIA'S eyelids]*

ORIGINAL

# ACT II, SCENE 2

In another part of the woods outside Athens.

*[TITANIA, Queen of the Fairies, enters with her company.]*

**TITANIA**     For twenty seconds, let's enjoy a fairy song and circle dance before departing. Some of you must kill canker-worms in the musk rose buds. Some of you must battle bats and take their leathery wings to make coats for elves. Some of you must drive off the noisy owl, who hoots at our frolics. Sing me to sleep. Then, while I rest, do what I assigned you. *[The FAIRIES sing.]*

**FIRST FAIRY**     *[The FAIRY sings]* Go away, spotted snakes with forked tongues and prickly hedgehogs. Do no harm, you sala-manders and slugs. Stay away from our Fairy Queen.

**CHORUS**     *[The fairy chorus sings.]* Nightingale, add melody to our sweet lullaby. Lulla, lulla, lullaby; lulla, lulla, lullaby. Allow no harm or magic to threaten Titania. Good night with a soothing melody.

**SECOND FAIRY**     *[The SECOND FAIRY sings.]* Go away, web-spinning spi-ders. You daddy longlegs, stay away. Black beetles, don't come this way. Do no damage to Titania, you worm or snail.

**CHORUS**     *[The chorus of FAIRIES sings.]* Melodious nightingale, etc. *[TITANIA falls asleep.]*

**FIRST FAIRY**     Let's go. She is safe. One fairy stand guard. *[The FAIRIES depart. OBERON enters and drops the pansy juice on TITANIA's eyelids.]*

TRANSLATION

| | |
|---|---|
| **OBERON** | What thou seest when thou dost wake, |
| | Do it for thy true love take; |
| | Love and languish for his sake. |
| | Be it ounce, or cat, or bear,                                    30 |
| | Pard, or boar with bristled hair, |
| | In thy eye that shall appear |
| | When thou wak'st, it is thy dear; |
| | Wake when some vile thing is near. |
| | *[Exit]* |
| | *[Enter LYSANDER and HERMIA]* |
| **LYSANDER** | Fair love, you faint with wandering in the wood,     35 |
| | And, to speak troth, I have forgot our way. |
| | We'll rest us, Hermia, if you think it good, |
| | And tarry for the comfort of the day. |
| **HERMIA** | Be it so, Lysander: find you out a bed, |
| | For I upon this bank will rest my head.                   40 |
| **LYSANDER** | One turf shall serve as pillow for us both; |
| | One heart, one bed, two bosoms, and one troth. |
| **HERMIA** | Nay, good Lysander; for my sake, my dear, |
| | Lie farther off yet, do not lie so near. |
| **LYSANDER** | O, take the sense, sweet, of my innocence;           45 |
| | Love takes the meaning in love's conference. |
| | I mean that my heart unto yours is knit; |
| | So that but one heart we can make of it: |
| | Two bosoms interchained with an oath; |
| | So then two bosoms and a single troth.                  50 |
| | Then by your side no bed-room me deny; |
| | For lying so, Hermia, I do not lie. |
| **HERMIA** | Lysander riddles very prettily: |
| | Now much beshrew my manners and my pride |
| | If Hermia meant to say Lysander lied.                     55 |
| | But, gentle friend, for love and courtesy |
| | Lie further off, in human modesty. |
| | Such separation as may well be said |
| | Becomes a virtuous bachelor and a maid: |
| | So far be distant; and good night, sweet friend:      60 |
| | Thy love ne'er alter till thy sweet life end! |

| | |
|---|---|
| OBERON | Whatever you see when you wake up you will adore like your true love. For him, you will worship and wither. Whether you see a lynx, wildcat, bear, leopard, or bristly hog. Whatever strikes your eye when you arise will be dear to you. Wake up when some vile animal approaches. *[When OBERON departs, LYSANDER and HERMIA appear.]* |
| LYSANDER | Sweetheart, you are weary from walking in the woods. To be truthful, I have lost the way. We will rest here, Hermia, if you agree, and wait until daylight. |
| HERMIA | Yes, Lysander, let's rest. You find a sleeping place while I rest on this bank. |
| LYSANDER | We will share a spot. One love, one bed, two hearts, and one vow. |
| HERMIA | No, dear Lysander. For my reputation, dear, sleep apart from me. |
| LYSANDER | Dear Hermia, I meant no damage to your modesty. Lovers share the same thought when they talk. I meant that my affection is joined to yours. The union creates a single heart. Two hearts joined by a pledge of love. So two hearts become one unit. Don't send me away from your side. If I sleep next to you, Hermia, I will not harm you. |
| HERMIA | Lysander, you explain your meaning gracefully. Forgive me for implying that you are a liar. But, my love, for affection and courtesy, sleep away from me to preserve my reputation. Sleeping separately is appropriate for a well-meaning bachelor and a virgin. Sleep over there and good night, sweetheart. May your love last through all your life! |

ACT II

TRANSLATION

| | |
|---|---|
| **LYSANDER** | Amen, amen, to that fair prayer say I;<br>And then end life when I end loyalty!<br>Here is my bed. Sleep give thee all his rest! |
| **HERMIA** | With half that wish the wisher's eyes be pressed!    65<br>*[They sleep]*<br>*[Enter PUCK]* |
| **PUCK** | Through the forest have I gone,<br>But Athenian found I none,<br>On whose eyes I might approve<br>This flower's force in stirring love.<br>Night and silence—Who is here?    70<br>Weeds of Athens he doth wear:<br>This is he, my master said,<br>Despised the Athenian maid;<br>And here the maiden, sleeping sound<br>On the dank and dirty ground.    75<br>Pretty soul, she durst not lie<br>Near this lack-love, this kill-courtesy.<br>Churl, upon thy eyes I throw<br>All the power this charm doth owe.<br>*[He drops the juice on LYSANDER'S eyelids]*<br>When thou wak'st let love forbid    80<br>Sleep his seat on thy eyelid:<br>So, awake when I am gone;<br>For I must now to Oberon.<br>*[Exit]*<br>*[Enter DEMETRIUS and HELENA, running]* |
| **HELENA** | Stay, though thou kill me, sweet Demetrius. |
| **DEMETRIUS** | I charge thee, hence, and do not haunt me thus.    85 |
| **HELENA** | O, wilt thou darkling leave me? Do not so. |
| **DEMETRIUS** | Stay on thy peril; I alone will go.<br>*[Exit]* |

| | |
|---|---|
| LYSANDER | I agree. And may I die if I stop loving you! I will sleep here. Rest well! |
| HERMIA | You also sleep well! *[They fall asleep.] [PUCK enters.]* |
| PUCK | I have traveled the woods without finding an Athenian on whom to drop the magic juice of this pansy. It's a silent night. Who is this? He wears Athenian clothing. This is the man that Oberon said rejected the Athenian girl. And here is the maid, asleep on wet soil. She's a pretty girl. She shouldn't lie near this rude, unloving man. Bum, I put powerful pansy juice on your eyes. *[PUCK anoints LYSANDER'S eyes with blossom juice.]* When you wake up, you will love whatever creature you see. Arise after I leave. I must return to Oberon. *[PUCK departs.] [DEMETRIUS and HELENA run onstage.]* |

ACT II

| | |
|---|---|
| HELENA | Stop, you will kill me, sweet Demetrius. |
| DEMETRIUS | I demand that you leave me alone. |
| HELENA | Would you leave me in the dark? Please don't. |
| DEMETRIUS | Stay or risk harm. I will go on alone. *[DEMETRIUS departs.]* |

TRANSLATION

| HELENA | O, I am out of breath in this fond chase! |
| | The more my prayer, the lesser is my grace. |
| | Happy is Hermia, wheresoe'er she lies, | 90 |
| | For she hath blessed and attractive eyes. |
| | How came her eyes so bright? Not with salt tears— |
| | If so, my eyes are oftener washed than hers. |
| | No, no, I am as ugly as a bear; |
| | For beasts that meet me run away for fear: | 95 |
| | Therefore no marvel though Demetrius |
| | Do, as a monster, fly my presence thus. |
| | What wicked and dissembling glass of mine |
| | Made me compare with Hermia's sphery eyne? |
| | But who is here? Lysander, on the ground? | 100 |
| | Dead, or asleep? I see no blood, no wound. |
| | Lysander, if you live, good sir, awake. |

LYSANDER    *[Waking]* And run through fire I will for thy sweet sake.
            Transparent Helena! Nature shows art,
            That through thy bosom makes me see thy heart.    105
            Where is Demetrius? O, how fit a word
            Is that vile name to perish on my sword!

HELENA      Do not say so, Lysander; say not so.
            What though he love your Hermia? Lord, what though?
            Yet Hermia still loves you; then be content.    110

LYSANDER    Content with Hermia? No, I do repent
            The tedious minutes I with her have spent.
            Not Hermia but Helena I love.
            Who will not change a raven for a dove?
            The will of man is by his reason swayed;    115
            And reason says you are the worthier maid.
            Things growing are not ripe until their season;
            So I, being young, till now ripe not to reason;
            And touching now the point of human skill,
            Reason becomes the marshal to my will,    120
            And leads me to your eyes, where I o'erlook
            Love's stories, written in love's richest book.

| HELENA | I am out of breath from chasing my beloved! The more I pray to have Demetrius, the less God gives me. Hermia is lucky, wherever she is, to have blessedly beautiful eyes. Why are her eyes bright? Not from crying. If tears made eyes bright, I weep more often than she. But I am as ugly as a bear. I scare away wild animals. It is no wonder that Demetrius runs from me as though I were a monster. What evil mirror made me compare my eyes with Hermia's starry eyes? Who is this? Why is Lysander on the ground? Is he dead or asleep? I don't see blood or a wound. Lysander, if you are alive, wake up. |

ACT II

| LYSANDER | *[Awakening]* I would run through fire for your love, Helena. Helena, you are radiant! Nature lets me look through your exterior into your heart. Where is Demetrius? Oh, I am eager to kill him with my sword! |

| HELENA | Don't say that, Lysander, don't. Why should you care that he loves Hermia? Lord, what does it matter? Hermia loves only you. You should be satisfied. |

| LYSANDER | I should be satisfied with Hermia? No, I regret wasting my time with her. I love you, Helena, not Hermia. Who would not give up a black bird for a dove? Good sense controls my desire. I conclude that you are a more valuable girl. Love ripens like fruit. I was unripe until I developed good sense. Reason now controls my will. Reason leads me to you and to a love like those in books of romance. |

TRANSLATION

HELENA

Wherefore was I to this keen mockery born?
When at your hands did I deserve this scorn?
Is't not enough, is't not enough, young man,                 125
That I did never—no, nor never can—
Deserve a sweet look from Demetrius' eye,
But you must flout my insufficiency?
Good troth, you do me wrong, good sooth, you do
In such disdainful manner me to woo.                        130
But fare you well. Perforce I must confess,
I thought you lord of more true gentleness.
O, that a lady of one man refused
Should of another therefore be abused!
*[Exit]*

LYSANDER

She sees not Hermia. Hermia, sleep thou there,             135
And never mayst thou come Lysander near.
For, as a surfeit of the sweetest things
The deepest loathing to the stomach brings,
Or as the heresies that men do leave
Are hated most of those they did deceive,                  140
So thou, my surfeit and my heresy,
Of all be hated, but the most of me!
And, all my powers, address your love and might
To honour Helen, and to be her knight!
*[Exit]*

HERMIA

*[Waking]* Help me, Lysander, help me! Do thy best        145
To pluck this crawling serpent from my breast!
Ay me, for pity! What a dream was here!
Lysander, look how I do quake with fear!
Methought a serpent ate my heart away,
And you sat smiling at his cruel prey.                     150
Lysander! What, removed? Lysander! Lord!
What, out of hearing? Gone? No sound, no word?
Alack, where are you? Speak, an if you hear;
Speak, of all loves! I swoon almost with fear.
No? Then I well perceive you are not nigh:                 155
Either death or you I'll find immediately.
*[Exit]*

HELENA    Why is this happening to me? Why are you mocking me? Isn't it bad enough that you never flirted with me and never will? Do you have to make fun of my faults? You wrong me by courting me. But, goodbye. I admit that I admired your kindness. Oh, why would a woman whom Demetrius rejected be courted by Lysander! *[HELENA goes out.]*

LYSANDER    Helena didn't see Hermia. Hermia, sleep on. And stay away from Lysander. Just as eating too many sweets turns the stomach, so false beliefs seem most hated to those who once treasured them. So, my overfondness and my false love I hate more than anyone could! I pledge my love and energy to honor Helena. I would be her knight! *[LYSANDER goes out.]*

HERMIA    *[Awakening]* Lysander, help me! Pull this snake off my chest! Heaven help, what a nightmare! Lysander, I am trembling with fear! I dreamed that a snake ate my heart while you smiled. Lysander! Are you gone? Lysander, my lord! Have you left me without a sound or word? Where are you? Call if you can hear me. Speak to me! I feel faint with terror. No word? I know you must be gone. Either I will soon find you or I will die. *[HERMIA goes out.]*

# ACT III, SCENE I

The woods near Athens.

*[Enter the Clowns: QUINCE, SNUG, BOTTOM, FLUTE, SNOUT, and STARVELING]*

| | |
|---|---|
| **BOTTOM** | Are we all met? |
| **QUINCE** | Pat, pat; and here's a marvelous convenient place for our rehearsal. This green plot shall be our stage, this hawthorn brake our tiring-house, and we will do it in action, as we will do it before     5 the Duke. |
| **BOTTOM** | Peter Quince? |
| **QUINCE** | What sayest thou, bully Bottom? |
| **BOTTOM** | There are things in this comedy of 'Pyramus and Thisby' that will never please. First, Pyramus   10 must draw a sword to kill himself, which the ladies cannot abide. How answer you that? |
| **SNOUT** | By'r lakin, a parlous fear! |
| **STARVELING** | I believe we must leave the killing out, when all is done.   15 |
| **BOTTOM** | Not a whit. I have a device to make all well. Write me a prologue; and let the prologue seem to say we will do no harm with our swords, and that Pyramus is not killed indeed; and for the more better assurance, tell them that I Pyramus   20 am not Pyramus, but Bottom the weaver: this will put them out of fear. |
| **QUINCE** | Well, we will have such a prologue; and it shall be written in eight and six. |
| **BOTTOM** | No, make it two more; let it be written in   25 eight and eight. |
| **SNOUT** | Will not the ladies be afeard of the lion? |
| **STARVELING** | I fear it, I promise you. |

# ACT III, SCENE I

The woods outside the Greek city-state of Athens.

*[The players QUINCE, SNUG, BOTTOM, FLUTE, SNOUT, and STARVELING enter the stage.]*

| | |
|---|---|
| BOTTOM | Are we all here? |
| QUINCE | Right! Here's a good place to practice our play. This green lawn shall be the stage. This hawthorn grove will be the dressing room. We will perform the play just as we will before the Duke. |
| BOTTOM | Peter Quince? |
| QUINCE | What, good old Bottom? |
| BOTTOM | There are aspects of this comedy 'Pyramus and Thisby' that people won't like. First, Pyramus must hold his sword to stab himself. Female viewers won't like violence. What do you say to my advice? |
| SNOUT | By the Virgin Mary, a fearful scene! |
| STARVELING | I think we should omit violence from the whole play. |
| BOTTOM | Don't remove the scene. I know a way to smooth over it. Compose an introduction. Let the introduction say that we hurt no one with our swords. And state that Pyramus does not really die. Say that I am only playing Pyramus, but I'm really Bottom the weaver. The introduction will calm the audience. |
| QUINCE | Okay, I will include an introduction. I will compose it in eight-beat lines followed by six-beat lines. |
| BOTTOM | No, add two beats. Let it take the form of eight-beat lines followed by eight-beat lines. |
| SNOUT | Won't the lion terrify the women? |
| STARVELING | I am afraid so. |

ACT III

TRANSLATION

| | |
|---|---|
| **BOTTOM** | Masters, you ought to consider with yourselves to bring in—God shield us!—a lion among ladies is a most dreadful thing: for there is not a more fearful wildfowl than your lion living; and we ought to look to't. |
| **SNOUT** | Therefore another prologue must tell he is not a lion. |
| **BOTTOM** | Nay, you must name his name, and half his face must be seen through the lion's neck, and he himself must speak through, saying thus, or to the same defect, 'Ladies', or 'Fair ladies, I would wish you', or 'I would request you', or, 'I would entreat you, not to fear, not to tremble: my life for yours. If you think I come hither as a lion, it were pity of my life. No, I am no such thing; I am a man as other men are'—and there, indeed, let him name his name, and tell them plainly he is Snug the joiner. |
| **QUINCE** | Well, it shall be so. But there is two hard things; That is, to bring the moonlight into a chamber— for, you know, Pyramus and Thisby meet by moonlight. |
| **SNUG** | Doth the moon shine that night we play our play? |
| **BOTTOM** | A calendar, a calendar! Look in the almanac— find out moonshine, find out moonshine! |
| **QUINCE** | Yes, it doth shine that night. |
| **BOTTOM** | Why, then may you leave a casement of the great chamber window where we play open, and the moon may shine in at the casement. |
| **QUINCE** | Ay, or else one must come in with a bush of thorns and a lantern, and say he comes to dis- figure or to present the person of moonshine. Then there is another thing: we must have a wall in the great chamber; for Pyramus and Thisby, says the story, did talk through the chink of a wall. |
| **SNOUT** | You can never bring in a wall. What say you, Bottom? |

*30*

*35*

*40*

*45*

*50*

*55*

*60*

*65*

ORIGINAL

| | |
|---|---|
| BOTTOM | Workmen, you should reconsider whether to introduce—God help us!—a dreadful lion among women. There is no scarier wild bird than a lion. We should correct that part of the play. |
| SNOUT | Add another introduction to say that it is not really a lion. |
| BOTTOM | You must name the actor who plays the lion. Let half the actor's face show through the lion mask. The actor must speak through the mask. He should say, "Ladies" or "Fair ladies, I want you," or "I request that you" or "I beg you not to be scared or to shake. I would give my life to save yours. If you think I am a real lion, I give up living. I am not a lion. I am a human man." Let the actor give his real name. Speak straight out that he is Snug the furniture maker. |
| QUINCE | Okay. There are two more problems. There must be moonlight in the room. You know that Pyramus and Thisby meet in the moon's light. |
| SNUG | Will the moon be shining the night we give the play? |
| BOTTOM | Hand me a calendar! Look in the almanac—search for the phases of the moon! |
| QUINCE | Yes, the moon will shine on that night. |
| BOTTOM | Then open a window in the room where we perform the play. The moon's rays will come in at the window. |
| QUINCE | We could send in a player with a thorn bush and a lantern. We could say he symbolizes the moon's light. There is another problem. We need a wall on the stage. According to the myth, Pyramus and Thisby talked through a gap in the wall. |
| SNOUT | You can't set up a wall on stage. What do you think, Bottom? |

ACT III

TRANSLATION

BOTTOM    Some man or other must present Wall; and let
him have some plaster, or some loam, or some
rough-cast about him, to signify wall; and let
him hold his fingers thus, and through that                    70
cranny shall Pyramus and Thisby whisper.

QUINCE    If that may be, then all is well. Come, sit down,
Every mother's son, and rehearse your parts.
Pyramus, you begin: when you have spoken
your speech, enter into that brake; and so every               75
one according to his cue.
*[Enter PUCK behind]*

PUCK      What hempen homespuns have we swaggering here,
So near the cradle of the Fairy Queen?
What, a play toward! I'll be an auditor—
An actor too perhaps, if I see cause.                          80

QUINCE    Speak, Pyramus. Thisby, stand forth.

BOTTOM    *[as Pyramus]* Thisby, the flowers of odious savours sweet—

QUINCE    Odorous, odorous.

BOTTOM    *[as Pyramus]* —odours savours sweet:
So hath thy breath, my dearest Thisby dear.                    85
But hark, a voice! Stay thou but here awhile,
And by and by I will to thee appear.
*[Exit]*

PUCK      A stranger Pyramus than e'er played here!
*[Exit]*

FLUTE     Must I speak now?

QUINCE    Ay, marry, must you: for you must understand           90
he goes but to see a noise that he heard, and is to
come again.

FLUTE     *[as Thisby]* Most radiant Pyramus, most lily white of hue,
Of colour like the red rose on triumphant briar,
Most brisky juvenal, and eke most lovely Jew,                  95
As true as truest horse, that would never tire,
I'll meet thee, Pyramus, at Ninny's tomb—

QUINCE    'Ninus' tomb', man! Why, you must not speak
that yet; that you answer to Pyramus. You speak
all your part at once, cues, and all. Pyramus enter.           100
Your cue is past; it is 'never tire.'

| | |
|---|---|
| BOTTOM | A player must take the part of Wall. Cover him in plaster or dirt or pebbly surfacing to indicate a wall. Let him hold his fingers in a V. Pyramus and Thisby can whisper through the V. |
| QUINCE | If that works, we've solved the problem. Everybody sit down and rehearse your spoken lines. Pyramus, you begin. When you have said your part, enter the grove. Everybody follow on time. *[PUCK enters the stage behind the players.]* |
| PUCK | What homely peasants are strutting here near Titania's resting place? Well, a play in the process. I will listen. If I see a reason, I will take part in the action. |
| QUINCE | Pyramus, speak. Thisby, stand near him. |
| BOTTOM | *[BOTTOM, speaking Pyramus's lines]* Thisby, the blossom of odious smell— |
| QUINCE | Odorous, not odious. |
| BOTTOM | *[BOTTOM, speaking Pyramus's lines]*—sweet odors. Your breath is flowery sweet, dearest Thisby. Wait, I hear someone! Stay at the wall. Shortly, I will return. *[BOTTOM goes out.]* |
| PUCK | This is the strangest actor I've ever seen play Pyramus! *[PUCK goes out.]* |
| FLUTE | Is it my turn to speak? |
| QUINCE | Yes, you must. You see, Pyramus goes out to check on a noise, but he returns. |
| FLUTE | *[FLUTE playing the part of Thisby]* Pyramus, glowing white as a lily, the color of a red rose on a thorn. You are vigorously youthful and as handsome as a Jew, as loyal as an untiring horse. I'll wait for you, Pyramus, at Ninny's grave. |
| QUINCE | At the grave of Ninus, Babylon's founder, Flute. Don't say that line yet. That should be your reply to Pyramus. You are reading all your lines at once, including the cues. Pyramus enters here. Bottom, you missed your cue. You come in on "never tire." |

ACT III

| | |
|---|---|
| **FLUTE** | O—*[as Thisby]* As true as truest horse, that yet would never tire.<br>*[Enter PUCK, and BOTTOM with the ass head on]* |
| **BOTTOM** | *[as Pyramus]* If I were fair, Thisby, I were only thine. |
| **QUINCE** | O monstrous! O strange! We are haunted.                     105<br>Pray, masters! Fly, masters! Help!<br>*[Exeunt QUINCE, SNUG, FLUTE, SNOUT, and STARVELING]* |
| **PUCK** | I'll follow you; I'll lead you about a round,<br>Through bog, through bush, through brake, through briar;<br>Sometime a horse I'll be, sometime a hound,<br>A hog, a headless bear, sometime a fire;                     110<br>And neigh, and bark, and grunt, and roar, and burn,<br>Like horse, hound, hog, bear, fire, at every turn.<br>*[Exit]* |
| **BOTTOM** | Why do they run away? This is a knavery of<br>them to make me afeard.<br>*[Enter SNOUT]* |
| **SNOUT** | O Bottom, thou art changed! What do I see on thee?          115 |
| **BOTTOM** | What do you see? You see an ass-head of your<br>own, do you?<br>*[Re-enter QUINCE]* |
| **QUINCE** | Bless thee, Bottom, bless thee! Thou art translated!<br>*[Exit]* |
| **BOTTOM** | I see their knavery: this is to make an ass of<br>me; to fright me, if they could. But I will not stir          120<br>from this place, do what they can: I will walk up<br>and down here, and I will sing, that they shall<br>hear I am not afraid.<br>*[Sings]*<br>The woosel cock so black of hue,<br>With orange-tawny bill,                                        125<br>The throstle with his note so true,<br>The wren with little quill. |
| **TITANIA** | *[Waking]* What angel wakes me from my flowery bed? |

| | |
|---|---|
| FLUTE | Oh—*[FLUTE playing the part of Thisby]* as loyal as an untiring horse. *[PUCK precedes BOTTOM, who wears a donkey's head.]* |
| BOTTOM | *[BOTTOM playing the part of Pyramus]* To be honest, Thisby, I am all yours. |
| QUINCE | Oh, a monster! A strange being! It haunts us. Please, workman! Run, workers! Help! *[QUINCE, SNUG, FLUTE, SNOUT, and STARVELING run away.]* |
| PUCK | I will follow you, actors. I will mislead you in a circle through swamps, grove, fern, and briars. I will change shape from horse to bloodhound, to hog, headless bear, even flames. At each change, I will whinny, bark, grunt, growl, and crackle like horse, bloodhound, hog, bear, and flames. *[PUCK goes out.]* |
| BOTTOM | Why are the other actors running? This is a trick to scare me. *[SNOUT enters.]* |
| SNOUT | Oh, Bottom, you have changed! What is on your head? |
| BOTTOM | What does it look like? Have you dreamed up a donkey's head? *[QUINCE returns.]* |
| QUINCE | God help you, Bottom! You are changed! *[QUINCE goes out.]* |
| BOTTOM | I see their trickery. They're trying to make a fool of me. They would scare me if they could. But I won't let them scare me away. I will walk up and down the stage and sing to show I am not frightened. *[BOTTOM sings.]* The black bird has a brownish-orange bill. The thrush sings a clear note. The wren pipes out its song. |
| TITANIA | *[TITANIA awakens.]* What angel draws me out of my flowery sleeping place? |

ACT III

TRANSLATION

BOTTOM                *[Sings]* The finch, the sparrow, and the lark,
                      The plain-song cuckoo grey,                              130
                      Whose note full many a man doth mark,
                      And dares not answer nay—
                      for, indeed, who would set his wit to so foolish
                      a bird? Who would give a bird the lie, though
                      he cry 'cuckoo' never so?                                135

TITANIA               I pray thee, gentle mortal, sing again;
                      Mine ear is much enamoured of thy note.
                      So is mine eye enthralled to thy shape;
                      And thy fair virtue's force perforce doth move me,
                      On the first view, to say, to swear, I love thee.        140

BOTTOM                Methinks, mistress, you should have little reason
                      For that: and yet, to say the truth, reason and
                      love keep little company together now-a-days:
                      the more the pity that some honest neighbours
                      will not make them friends. Nay, I can gleek             145
                      upon occasion.

TITANIA               Thou art as wise as thou art beautiful.

BOTTOM                Not so, neither; but if I had wit enough to get
                      out of this wood, I have enough to serve mine own turn.

TITANIA               Out of this wood do not desire to go:                    150
                      Thou shalt remain here, whether thou wilt or no.
                      I am a spirit of no common rate,
                      The summer still doth tend upon my state;
                      And I do love thee: therefore, go with me,
                      I'll give thee fairies to attend on thee,                155
                      And they shall fetch thee jewels from the deep,
                      And sing, while thou on pressed flowers dost sleep;
                      And I will purge thy mortal grossness so
                      That thou shalt like an airy spirit go.
                      Peaseblossom, Cobweb, Moth, and Mustardseed!             160
                      *[Enter four fairies: PEASEBLOSSOM, COBWEB, MOTH, and,*
                      *MUSTARDSEED]*

PEASEBLOSSOM  Ready.

COBWEB                     And I.

MOTH                          And I.

MUSTARDSEED                            Where shall we go?

| | |
|---|---|
| **BOTTOM** | *[BOTTOM sings.]* The finch, sparrow, and lark and the gray cuckoo's simple notes alert many men, who can't deny the sound. Who would argue with the foolish cuckoo? Who would call a bird a liar, even though the bird plainly calls "cuckoo"? |
| **TITANIA** | Please, kind man, speak again. I am in love with your words. I can't take my eyes off you. From the first time I saw you, I loved you. |
| **BOTTOM** | Ma'am, you would have little call to love me. Truly, sanity and infatuation remain apart. It's a pity that no one can bring sanity and infatuation together. I am just joking. |
| **TITANIA** | You are as wise as you are handsome. |
| **BOTTOM** | No. If I were smart enough to leave the woods, that's all the wit I need. |
| **TITANIA** | Don't leave the woods. You will stay whether or not you want to. I am not an ordinary fairy. I control the summer. I love you, so go with me. I will give you fairies for servants. They will bring you gemstones. They will sing to you while you sleep on pressed blossoms. I will strip away your human form and turn you into a sprite. *[The four fairies enter.]* Peaseblossom, Spiderweb, Moth, and Mustardseed! |
| **PEASEBLOSSOM** | I'm ready. |
| **COBWEB** | Me, too. |
| **MOTH** | Me, too. |
| **MUSTARDSEED** | Where are you sending us? |

ACT III

TRANSLATION

| | |
|---|---|
| **TITANIA** | Be kind and courteous to this gentleman: |
| | Hop in his walks and gambol in his eyes; |
| | Feed him with apricocks and dewberries, |
| | With purple grapes, green figs, and mulberries;      165 |
| | The honey bags steal from the humble-bees, |
| | And, for night-tapers, crop their waxen thighs, |
| | And light them at the fiery glow-worm's eyes, |
| | To have my love to bed and to arise; |
| | And pluck the wings from painted butterflies      170 |
| | To fan the moonbeams from his sleeping eyes: |
| | Nod to him, elves, and do him courtesies. |
| **PEASEBLOSSOM** | Hail, mortal! |
| **COBWEB** | Hail! |
| **MOTH** | Hail!      175 |
| **MUSTARDSEED** | Hail! |
| **BOTTOM** | I cry your worships mercy, heartily. I beseech |
| | Your worship's name. |
| **COBWEB** | Cobweb. |
| **BOTTOM** | I shall desire you of more acquaintance, good      180 |
| | Master Cobweb. If I cut my finger, I shall make |
| | bold with you. Your name, honest gentleman? |
| **PEASEBLOSSOM** | Peaseblossom. |
| **BOTTOM** | I pray you, commend me to Mistress Squash, |
| | your mother, and to Master Peascod, your      185 |
| | father. Good Master Peaseblossom, I shall desire |
| | you of more acquaintance too. Your name, |
| | I beseech you, sir? |
| **MUSTARDSEED** | Mustardseed. |
| **BOTTOM** | Good Master Mustardseed, I know your patience      190 |
| | well: That same cowardly, giant-like ox- |
| | beef hath devoured many a gentleman of your |
| | house. I promise you, your kindred hath made |
| | my eyes water ere now. I desire you of more |
| | acquaintance, good Master Mustardseed.      195 |
| **TITANIA** | Come, wait upon him. Lead him to my bower. |
| | The moon, methinks, looks with a watery eye, |
| | And when she weeps, weeps every little flower, |
| | Lamenting some enforced chastity. |
| | Tie up my love's tongue, bring him silently.      200 |
| | *[Exeunt]* |

ORIGINAL

| | |
|---|---|
| TITANIA | Be kind and courteous to Bottom. Hop along his path and frolic for him to enjoy. Feed him apricots, blackberries, purple grapes, green figs, and mulberries. Steal honey from bumblebees. For bedside candles, cut the wax from the bees' legs. Light them with a lightning bug's eyes at bedtime and morning. Pluck the wings from bright-colored butterflies to fan away the sleep from his eyes. Be agreeable, fairies, and do good deeds for him. |
| PEASEBLOSSOM | Hello, human! |
| COBWEB | Hello! |
| MOTH | Hello! |
| MUSTARDSEED | Hello! |
| BOTTOM | I beg your kindness with all my heart. I ask your name. |
| COBWEB | I am Spiderweb. |
| BOTTOM | I can make use of you, Spiderweb. If I cut my finger, I will stop the bleeding with you. What is your name, sir? |
| PEASEBLOSSOM | I am Peaseblossom. |
| BOTTOM | Please send my greetings to your mother, Mrs. Green Pea, and your father, Mr. Ripe Pea. Mr. Peaseblossom, I can also make use of you. What is your name, sir? |
| MUSTARDSEED | I am Mustardseed. |
| BOTTOM | Mr. Mustardseed, I know what you are good for. People eat mustard with beef roasts. Mustard makes my eyes water. I would like to know you better, Mr. Mustardseed. |
| TITANIA | You fairies serve Bottom. Lead him to my quarters. The moon looks like she is weeping. When the moon cries, blossoms weep. The flowers regret having their virginity violated. Silence Bottom and bring him along. *[They all depart.]* |

ACT III

# ACT III, SCENE 2

## Another part of the woods.

*[Enter OBERON, King of the Fairies]*

| | | |
|---|---|---|
| **OBERON** | I wonder if Titania be awaked; | |
| | Then, what it was that next came in her eye, | |
| | Which she must dote on in extremity. | |
| | *[Enter PUCK]* | |
| | Here comes my messenger. How now, mad spirit? | |
| | What night-rule now about this haunted grove? | 5 |
| | | |
| **PUCK** | My mistress with a monster is in love. | |
| | Near to her close and consecrated bower, | |
| | While she was in her dull and sleeping hour, | |
| | A crew of patches, rude mechanicals, | |
| | That work for bread upon Athenian stalls, | 10 |
| | Were met together to rehearse a play | |
| | Intended for great Theseus' nuptial day. | |
| | The shallowest thickskin of that barren sort | |
| | Who Pyramus presented in their sport, | |
| | Forsook his scene and entered in a brake, | 15 |
| | When I did him at this advantage take: | |
| | An ass's nole I fixed on his head. | |
| | Anon, his Thisby must be answered, | |
| | And forth my mimic comes. When they him spy— | |
| | As wild geese that the creeping fowler eye, | 20 |
| | Or russet-pated choughs, many in sort, | |
| | Rising and cawing at the gun's report, | |
| | Sever themselves and madly sweep the sky— | |
| | So at his sight away his fellows fly, | |
| | And at our stamp here, o'er and o'er one falls; | 25 |
| | He 'Murder!' cries, and help from Athens calls. | |
| | Their sense thus weak, lost with their fears, thus strong, | |
| | Made senseless things begin to do them wrong, | |
| | For briars and thorns at their apparel snatch, | |
| | Some sleeves, some hats; from yielders all things catch. | 30 |
| | I led them on in this distracted fear, | |
| | And left sweet Pyramus translated there; | |
| | When in that moment, so it came to pass, | |
| | Titania waked, and straightway loved an ass. | |

ORIGINAL

# ACT III, SCENE 2

In another part of the forest outside of Athens.

*[OBERON, King of the Fairies, enters.]*

OBERON
I wonder if Titania is awake. Whatever she first sees, she will fall madly in love with. *[PUCK arrives.]* Here comes my messenger. How are you, spirit? What night fun will take place in the woods?

PUCK
Titania is in love with a monster. Near her secret quarters, while she was asleep, a bunch of clowns, ignorant laborers that earn their living in Athenian shops, gathered to practice a play to honor Theseus's wedding to Hippolyta. The densest one of the players acts the part of Pyramus. He left the stage and entered a grove, where I found him. I put a donkey's head on his head. Soon, Pyramus will return to say his lines to Thisby. When the workers see Bottom, they will run away like wild geese or red-headed jackdaws flapping away into the sky at the sound of the hunter's gun. And at our tread, one by one, the men will fall. Bottom will cry "Murder!" and yell to Athens for protection. Thus weakened by fear, the players will sink into confusion. Briars and stickers will grab at their sleeves and hats, and will seize the weaklings. I created this terror. I left Pyramus on this spot. In that instant, Titania happened to arise and fall in love with a donkey.

ACT III

| | | |
|---|---|---|
| **OBERON** | This falls out better than I could devise. | 35 |
| | But hast thou yet latched the Athenian's eyes | |
| | With the love juice, as I did bid thee do? | |
| | | |
| **PUCK** | I took him sleeping—that is finished too— | |
| | And the Athenian woman by his side, | |
| | That, when he waked, of force she must be eyed. | 40 |
| | *[Enter DEMETRIUS and HERMIA]* | |
| | | |
| **OBERON** | Stand close; this is the same Athenian. | |
| | | |
| **PUCK** | This is the woman, but not this the man. | |
| | | |
| **DEMETRIUS** | O, why rebuke you him that loves you so? | |
| | Lay breath so bitter on your bitter foe. | |
| | | |
| **HERMIA** | Now I but chide, but I should use thee worse, | 45 |
| | For thou, I fear, hast given me cause to curse. | |
| | If thou hast slain Lysander in his sleep, | |
| | Being o'er shoes in blood, plunge in the deep, | |
| | And kill me too. | |
| | The sun was not so true unto the day | 50 |
| | As he to me: would he have stol'n away | |
| | From sleeping Hermia? I'll believe as soon | |
| | This whole earth may be bored, and that the moon | |
| | May through the centre creep and so displease | |
| | Her brother's noontide with th' Antipodes. | 55 |
| | It cannot be but thou hast murdered him. | |
| | So should a murderer look: so dead, so grim. | |
| | | |
| **DEMETRIUS** | So should the murdered look, and so should I, | |
| | Pierced through the heart with your stern cruelty; | |
| | Yet you, the murderer, look as bright, as clear, | 60 |
| | As yonder Venus in her glimmering sphere. | |
| | | |
| **HERMIA** | What's this to my Lysander? Where is he? | |
| | Ah, good Demetrius, wilt thou give him me? | |
| | | |
| **DEMETRIUS** | I had rather give his carcass to my hounds. | |
| | | |
| **HERMIA** | Out, dog! Out, cur! Thou driv'st me past the bounds | 65 |
| | Of maiden's patience. Hast thou slain him, then? | |
| | Henceforth be never numbered among men! | |
| | Oh. Once tell true; tell true, even for my sake: | |
| | Durst thou have looked upon him being awake? | |
| | And hast thou killed him sleeping? O brave touch! | 70 |
| | Could not a worm, an adder, do so much? | |
| | An adder did it; for with doubler tongue | |
| | Than thine, thou serpent, never adder stung. | |

| OBERON | This is even better than I had hoped. Have you also anointed the eyelids of the Athenian as I commanded? |
|---|---|
| PUCK | I found him asleep. I did what you said. The Athenian immediately fell in love with the first woman he saw. *[DEMETRIUS and HERMIA enter.]* |
| OBERON | Stay here. This is the Athenian. |
| PUCK | This is the woman, but not the man I anointed. |
| DEMETRIUS | How can you reject a man who truly loves you? How can you utter bitter words on him like an enemy. |
| HERMIA | I am only scolding, but I could do something worse. You give me good reason to swear. If you murdered Lysander in his sleep, you are already soaked in blood, so kill me too. He is more faithful to me than the sun is to daylight. Would Lysander have crept away from me? I would sooner believe that the moon could sneak through a hole in the earth and interrupt noon on the opposite side of the world. I believe you murdered him. A killer would look as emotionless and evil as you. |
| DEMETRIUS | I look just like a killer because you wound my heart. But you still look as gorgeous as Venus in the sky. |
| HERMIA | What does this have to do with Lysander? Where is he? Please, Demetrius, show me where he is. |
| DEMETRIUS | I would rather feed his carcass to my dogs. |
| HERMIA | Away with you, stray hound! You force me beyond a woman's patience. Did you kill him? May you never be called a man! Tell me the truth, for my sake. Did you see him after he awoke? Did you kill him while he slept? Oh, that was brave of you! Wouldn't a snake or serpent do the same? A snake did do it. No serpent could have a more deceptive tongue than yours. |

ACT III

| | |
|---|---|
| **DEMETRIUS** | You spend your passion on a misprised mood: |
| | I am not guilty of Lysander's blood, 75 |
| | Nor is he dead, for aught that I can tell. |
| **HERMIA** | I pray thee, tell me, then, that he is well. |
| **DEMETRIUS** | And if I could, what should I get therefore? |
| **HERMIA** | A privilege never to see me more. |
| | And from thy hated presence part I so. 80 |
| | See me no more, whether he be dead or no. |
| | *[Exit]* |
| **DEMETRIUS** | There is no following her in this fierce vein; |
| | Here, therefore, for a while I will remain. |
| | So sorrow's heaviness doth heavier grow |
| | For debt that bankrupt sleep doth sorrow owe; 85 |
| | Which now in some slight measure it will pay, |
| | If for his tender here I make some stay. |
| | *[Lies down]* |
| **OBERON** | What hast thou done? Thou hast mistaken quite, |
| | And laid the love-juice on some true-love's sight: |
| | Of thy misprision must perforce ensue 90 |
| | Some true love turned, and not a false turned true. |
| **PUCK** | Then fate o'er-rules, that, one man holding troth, |
| | A million fail, confounding oath on oath. |
| **OBERON** | About the wood go, swifter than the wind, |
| | And Helena of Athens look thou find. 95 |
| | All fancy-sick she is, and pale of cheer, |
| | With sighs of love, that costs the fresh blood dear. |
| | By some illusion see thou bring her here; |
| | I'll charm his eyes against she do appear. |
| **PUCK** | I go, I go; look how I go, 100 |
| | Swifter than arrow from the Tartar's bow! |
| | *[Exit]* |

| | |
|---|---|
| **DEMETRIUS** | You waste your anger on a faulty impression. I didn't kill Lysander. For all I know, he is still alive. |
| **HERMIA** | Oh please tell me that he is not hurt. |
| **DEMETRIUS** | What would you give me if I could reassure you? |
| **HERMIA** | I would reward you by going away. I would never see you again. Whatever the outcome, I will leave your sight. *[She departs.]* |
| **DEMETRIUS** | There is no reason to follow her when she is so mad. I will stay here for a while. My sadness will increase until I get some sleep. I will feel better if I stay here and rest. *[DEMETRIUS lies down.]* |
| **OBERON** | Puck, what have you done? You put the magic pansy juice on the wrong person. Because of your error, you ruined true love and produced a false affection. |
| **PUCK** | Fate rules everything. Only one man in a million keeps his promise to a lover. |
| **OBERON** | Hurry like the wind through the woods. Locate Helena of Athens. She is lovesick and pale. Her loving sighs steal away her color. Use magic to bring her here. I will put a spell on Demetrius until she returns. |
| **PUCK** | I fly away swifter than a Turk's arrow! *[PUCK departs.]* |

ACT III

TRANSLATION

| | | |
|---|---|---|
| **OBERON** | Flower of this purple dye, | |
| | Hit with Cupid's archery, | |
| | Sink in apple of his eye! | |
| | *[He drops the juice on DEMETRIUS' eyelids]* | |
| | When his love he doth espy, | 105 |
| | Let her shine as gloriously | |
| | As the Venus of the sky. | |
| | When thou wak'st, if she be by, | |
| | Beg of her for remedy. | |
| | *[Enter PUCK]* | |
| **PUCK** | Captain of our fairy band, | 110 |
| | Helena is here at hand, | |
| | And the youth mistook by me, | |
| | Pleading for a lover's fee. | |
| | Shall we their fond pageant see? | |
| | Lord, what fools these mortals be! | 115 |
| **OBERON** | Stand aside. The noise they make | |
| | Will cause Demetrius to awake. | |
| **PUCK** | Then will two at once woo one. | |
| | That must needs be sport alone; | |
| | And those things do best please me | 120 |
| | That befall prepost'rously. | |
| | *[Enter LYSANDER and HELENA]* | |
| **LYSANDER** | Why should you think that I should woo in scorn? | |
| | Scorn and derision never come in tears. | |
| | Look when I vow, I weep; and vows so born, | |
| | In their nativity all truth appears. | 125 |
| | How can these things in me seem scorn to you, | |
| | Bearing the badge of faith to prove them true? | |
| **HELENA** | You do advance your cunning more and more. | |
| | When truth kills truth, O devilish-holy fray! | |
| | These vows are Hermia's. Will you give her o'er? | 130 |
| | Weigh oath with oath, and you will nothing weigh: | |
| | Your vows to her and me, put in two scales, | |
| | Will even weigh, and both as light as tales. | |
| **LYSANDER** | I had no judgment when to her I swore. | |
| **HELENA** | Nor none, in my mind, now you give her o'er. | 135 |
| **LYSANDER** | Demetrius loves her, and he loves not you. | |

| OBERON | Purple pansy that Cupid struck with an arrow, drop juice on Demetrius's eyelid! *[He drips the pansy juice on DEMETRIUS's eyelids.]* When he sees his love, let her look like Venus in the sky. When you awaken, Demetrius, if she is near, beg her pardon. *[PUCK returns.]* |
|---|---|
| PUCK | Oberon, captain of the fairies, Helena is coming. Demetrius, the man I misidentified, begs once more for her love. Shall we watch them reunite? Lord, humans are silly! |
| OBERON | Stand over there. Hermia will awaken Demetrius. |
| PUCK | They will soon be a couple again. This should be fun. I enjoy events caused by confusion. *[LYSANDER and HELENA enter.]* |
| LYSANDER | Why do you think I make fun of you? I would weep while I mock you. See, I weep when I pledge my love. Promises spoken with tears are true. Why do my words seem deceptive when they come with tears? |
| HELENA | You become sneakier. When you court me like you courted Hermia, you commit a devilish sin! You said these words to Hermia. Are you giving her up? Your two vows—to me and to her—are worthless. Place your pledges on a scale. They weigh the same as lies. |
| LYSANDER | I was wrong when I courted her. |
| HELENA | You are wrong to give her up. |
| LYSANDER | Demetrius loves Hermia. He doesn't love you. |

ACT III

TRANSLATION

| | |
|---|---|
| **DEMETRIUS** | *[Waking]* O Helen, goddess, nymph, perfect, divine!<br>To what, my love, shall I compare thine eyne?<br>Crystal is muddy. O, how ripe in show<br>Thy lips, those kissing cherries, tempting grow!     140<br>That pure congealed white, high Taurus' snow,<br>Fanned with the eastern wind, turns to a crow<br>When thou hold'st up thy hand. O, let me kiss<br>This princess of pure white, this seal of bliss! |
| **HELENA** | O spite! O hell! I see you all are bent     145<br>To set against me for your merriment.<br>If you were civil, and knew courtesy,<br>You would not do me thus much injury.<br>Can you not hate me, as I know you do,<br>But you must join in souls to mock me too?     150<br>If you were men, as men you are in show,<br>You would not use a gentle lady so,<br>To vow, and swear, and superpraise my parts,<br>When I am sure you hate me with your hearts.<br>You both are rivals, and love Hermia;     155<br>And now both rivals, to mock Helena.<br>A trim exploit, a manly enterprise,<br>To conjure tears up in a poor maid's eyes<br>With your derision! None of noble sort<br>Would so offend a virgin, and extort     160<br>A poor soul's patience, all to make you sport. |
| **LYSANDER** | You are unkind, Demetrius. Be not so.<br>For you love Hermia: this you know I know.<br>And here, with all good will, with all my heart,<br>In Hermia's love I yield you up my part;     165<br>And yours of Helena to me bequeath,<br>Whom I do love and will do till my death. |
| **HELENA** | Never did mockers waste more idle breath. |
| **DEMETRIUS** | Lysander, keep thy Hermia; I will none.<br>If e'er I loved her, all that love is gone.     170<br>My heart to her but as guest-wise sojourned;<br>And now to Helen is it home returned,<br>There to remain. |
| **LYSANDER** |                 Helen, it is not so. |
| **DEMETRIUS** | Disparage not the faith thou dost not know,<br>Lest, to thy peril, thou aby it dear.     175<br>Look where thy love comes: yonder is thy dear.<br>*[Enter HERMIA]* |

| | |
|---|---|
| **DEMETRIUS** | *[DEMETRIUS awakens.]* Oh Helena, goddess, elf, perfect and sacred woman! What compares to your eyes? Crystal looks like mud. Your lips tempt me like ripe cherries. The windblown snow of the Turkish mountains looks black when placed alongside your hand. Let me kiss this pure princess, my joy! |
| **HELENA** | Oh meanness! Oh hell! You are all plotting to make a joke of me. If you had manners, you wouldn't mistreat me this way. Can't you just hate me without plotting to laugh at me too? If you were gentlemen, as you appear to be, you wouldn't mistreat a lady. You court and pledge and overpraise me when I know you despise me. Both of you love Hermia. You both ridicule me. This is no gentlemanly prank, to make a girl cry. No nobleman would insult a girl and try her patience for fun. |
| **LYSANDER** | Don't be mean, Demetrius. I know you love Hermia. I heartily give up Hermia to you. Give me Helena, whom I will love until I die. |
| **HELENA** | Never have tricksters wasted more words. |
| **DEMETRIUS** | Lysander, you keep Hermia. I don't want her. Even if I did love her, that love has ended. My affection was only temporary. I have returned to Helena and will never part from her. |
| **LYSANDER** | Helena, say it isn't so. |
| **DEMETRIUS** | Don't ridicule a loyalty you know nothing about. You may pay a terrible price. Look, your girlfriend is coming. There she is. *[HERMIA enters.]* |

ACT III

TRANSLATION

| | |
|---|---|
| **HERMIA** | Dark night, that from the eye his function takes, |
| | The ear more quick of apprehension makes; |
| | Wherein it doth impair the seeing sense, |
| | It pays the hearing double recompense: 180 |
| | Thou art not by mine eye, Lysander, found; |
| | Mine ear, I thank it, brought me to thy sound. |
| | But why unkindly didst thou leave me so? |
| **LYSANDER** | Why should he stay whom love doth press to go? |
| **HERMIA** | What love could press Lysander from my side? 185 |
| **LYSANDER** | Lysander's love, that would not let him bide: |
| | Fair Helena, who more engilds the night |
| | Than all yon fiery oes and eyes of light. |
| | Why seek'st thou me? Could not this make thee know |
| | The hate I bare thee made me leave thee so? 190 |
| **HERMIA** | You speak not as you think; it cannot be. |
| **HELENA** | Lo, she is one of this confederacy! |
| | Now I perceive they have conjoined all three |
| | To fashion this false sport in spite of me. |
| | Injurious Hermia! Most ungrateful maid, 195 |
| | Have you conspired, have you with these contrived, |
| | To bait me with this foul derision? |
| | Is all the counsel that we two have shared, |
| | The sisters' vows, the hours that we have spent, |
| | When we have chid the hasty-footed time 200 |
| | For parting us,—O, is all forgot? |
| | All schooldays' friendship, childhood innocence? |
| | We, Hermia, like two artificial gods, |
| | Have with our needles created both one flower, |
| | Both on one sampler, sitting on one cushion, 205 |
| | Both warbling of one song, both in one key; |
| | As if our hands, our sides, voices, and minds |
| | Had been incorporate. So we grew together, |
| | Like to a double cherry, seeming parted; |
| | But yet an union in partition, 210 |
| | Two lovely berries moulded on one stem; |
| | So, with two seeming bodies, but one heart; |
| | Two of the first, like coats in heraldry, |
| | Due but to one, and crowned with one crest. |
| | And will you rent our ancient love asunder, 215 |
| | To join with men in scorning your poor friend? |
| | It is not friendly, 'tis not maidenly: |
| | Our sex, as well as I, may chide you for it, |
| | Though I alone do feel the injury. |

| | |
|---|---|
| HERMIA | I hear better in the dark than I see. Although I can't see, I hear Lysander twice as well. Although I can't see Lysander, I hear you. Why did you abandon me? |

| | |
|---|---|
| LYSANDER | Why should I stay with you when I love someone else? |
| HERMIA | What affection takes you away from me? |
| LYSANDER | My love for someone else would not let me stay. Helena shines brighter in the night than stars. Why do you pursue me? Don't you realize that I hate you? |

| | |
|---|---|
| HERMIA | You don't mean it. It can't be. |
| HELENA | Aha, Hermia is part of this mockery! All three join in making fun of me. Wicked Hermia! Disloyal girl, have you plotted with them to torment me for fun? Have you forgotten how we shared secrets like sisters, how we regretted having to end our time together? Have you forgotten our childhood friendship, our girlish ways? We sat on one pillow and embroidered a flower on our needlework while singing the same song. We worked as though our hands, bodies, voices, and thoughts were one person. We grew together like a double cherry. We were like two cherries on one stem. We were two bodies with one heart. Like coats of arms, which crown a couple as one family. Will you destroy our friendship by joining Lysander and Demetrius in jeering at me? Your behavior is cruel, unladylike. All women will scold you for the cruelty I suffer. |

ACT III

| HERMIA | I am amazed at your passionate words: | 220 |
| | I scorn you not; it seems that you scorn me. | |
| | | |
| HELENA | Have you not set Lysander, as in scorn, | |
| | To follow me, and praise my eyes and face? | |
| | And made your other love, Demetrius, | |
| | Who even but now did spurn me with his foot, | 225 |
| | To call me goddess, nymph, divine, and rare, | |
| | Precious, celestial? Wherefore speaks he this | |
| | To her he hates? And wherefore doth Lysander | |
| | Deny your love, so rich within his soul, | |
| | And tender me, forsooth, affection, | 230 |
| | But by your setting on, by your consent? | |
| | What though I be not so in grace as you, | |
| | So hung upon with love, so fortunate, | |
| | But miserable most, to love unloved: | |
| | This you should pity rather than despise. | 235 |
| | | |
| HERMIA | I understand not what you mean by this. | |
| | | |
| HELENA | Ay, do! Persever, counterfeit sad looks, | |
| | Make mouths upon me when I turn my back, | |
| | Wink each at other; hold the sweet jest up. | |
| | This sport, well carried, shall be chronicled. | 240 |
| | If you have any pity, grace, or manners, | |
| | You would not make me such an argument. | |
| | But fare ye well: 'tis partly my own fault; | |
| | Which death, or absence, soon shall remedy. | |
| | | |
| LYSANDER | Stay, gentle Helena; hear my excuse; | 245 |
| | My love, my life, my soul, fair Helena! | |
| | | |
| HELENA | O excellent! | |
| | | |
| HERMIA | *[To LYSANDER]* Sweet, do not scorn her so. | |
| | | |
| DEMETRIUS | *[To LYSANDER]* If she cannot entreat, I can compel. | |
| | | |
| LYSANDER | Thou canst compel no more than she entreat; | |
| | Thy threats have no more strength than her weak prayers. | 250 |
| | Helen, I love thee; by my life I do. | |
| | I swear by that which I will lose for thee | |
| | To prove him false that says I love thee not. | |
| | | |
| DEMETRIUS | *[To HELENA]* I say I love thee more than he can do. | |
| | | |
| LYSANDER | If thou say so, withdraw, and prove it too. | 255 |

ORIGINAL

| | |
|---|---|
| HERMIA | I am bewildered by your charge. I am not laughing at you. You are mocking me. |
| HELENA | Didn't you send Lysander to pursue and court me? to compliment my eyes and face? Didn't you send Demetrius, who once abandoned me, to call me goddess, elf, perfect and precious, heavenly woman? Why would he say that to someone he hates? Why would Lysander abandon you, whom he cherished in his soul? Why would he offer me his love unless you told him to do it? Even though I am not so pretty, beloved, and lucky, why should I be made miserable? You should feel sorry for me rather than despise me. |
| HERMIA | I don't understand any of this. |
| HELENA | Yes, you do. Go on, pretend to be sorry for me. Smirk at me behind my back. Wink at each other and enjoy the joke. This game, so well played, will make history. If you have any sympathy, generosity, or courtesy, you would stop teasing me. Goodbye. It is partly my fault. I will end this game by dying or leaving you. |
| LYSANDER | Don't go, Helena. Hear my reason. You are my love, my life, my spirit, beautiful Helena! |
| HELENA | Not again! |
| HERMIA | [HERMIA to LYSANDER] Sweetheart, don't ridicule Helena. |
| DEMETRIUS | [DEMETRIUS to LYSANDER] If Hermia can't entice you to stop, I'll make you stop hounding Helena. |
| LYSANDER | You can't force me any more than she can beg me to stop. Your threats are no stronger than her pleas. I love you, Helena. I swear on my life. I swear by the loss of you to anybody who proves me a liar. |
| DEMETRIUS | [DEMETRIUS to HELENA] I love you more than Lysander does. |
| LYSANDER | If you think that, step aside and prove it. |

ACT III

TRANSLATION

| | |
|---|---|
| **DEMETRIUS** | Quick, come— |
| **HERMIA** | Lysander, whereto tends all this? |
| **LYSANDER** | Away, you Ethiope! |
| **DEMETRIUS** | No, no, sir, |

Seem to break loose; take on as you would follow,
But yet come not. You are a tame man, go.

**LYSANDER**      Hang off, thou cat, thou burr! Vile thing, let loose,      260
Or I will shake thee from me like a serpent.

**HERMIA**      Why are you grown so rude? What change is this,
Sweet love?

**LYSANDER**                Thy love! Out, tawny Tartar, out!
Out, loathed medicine! O hated potion, hence!

**HERMIA**      Do you not jest?

**HELENA**                Yes, sooth; and so do you.      265

**LYSANDER**      Demetrius, I will keep my word with thee.

**DEMETRIUS**      I would I had your bond; for I perceive
A weak bond holds you; I'll not trust your word.

**LYSANDER**      What! Should I hurt her, strike her, kill her dead?
Although I hate her, I'll not harm her so.      270

**HERMIA**      What! Can you do me greater harm than hate?
Hate me? Wherefore? O me! What news, my love?
Am not I Hermia? Are not you Lysander?
I am as fair now as I was erewhile.
Since night you loved me; yet since night you left me:      275
Why then, you left me—O, the gods forbid!—
In earnest, shall I say?

**LYSANDER**                Ay, by my life;
And never did desire to see thee more.
Therefore be out of hope, of question, doubt,
Be certain, nothing truer; 'tis no jest      280
That I do hate thee and love Helena.

**HERMIA**      *[To HELENA]* O me! You juggler! You cankerblossom!
You thief of love! What, have you come by night,
And stol'n my love's heart from him?

| | |
|---|---|
| DEMETRIUS | Come fight me now. |
| HERMIA | Lysander, what will a fight prove? |
| LYSANDER | Away, you African woman! |
| DEMETRIUS | No, Lysander, you pretend to part with Hermia. You pretend you want a fight, but you stay here. You are a coward. Off with you. |
| LYSANDER | Let go of me, you cat, you sticker! Let me go or I will yank you free like a snake. |
| HERMIA | Why have you changed? Sweetheart, what makes you so rude? |
| LYSANDER | Your clinging to me! Go away, dark Turk, go! Away, bitter taste! Oh, hateful drink, go away! |
| HERMIA | Are you teasing me? |
| HELENA | Yes, he is, and you are teasing me. |
| LYSANDER | Demetrius, I will keep my promise to fight you. |
| DEMETRIUS | I wish I had your promise in writing. You pledge a weak vow. I can't trust your word. |
| LYSANDER | Should I harm Hermia, hit her, kill her to prove myself honest? Although I hate her, I won't harm her just to prove my point. |
| HERMIA | What worse harm can you do to me than to hate me? Why do you hate me? Oh, no! What has changed, my love? Aren't I Hermia? Are you still Lysander? I look the same as I did yesterday. You loved me last night. You left me during the night. Why, god forbid, did you reject me? |
| LYSANDER | I vow on my life that I abandoned you. I don't ever want to see you again. So, accept my desertion as unquestionable, certain, sure. It is no joke that I hate you and love Helena. |
| HERMIA | *[HERMIA to HELENA]* Oh, you fraud! You cankerworm! You man-stealer! Why did you come in the night and steal away Lysander's heart? |

ACT III

TRANSLATION

| | |
|---|---|
| **HELENA** | Fine, i' faith! |
| | Have you no modesty, no maiden shame, 285 |
| | No touch of bashfulness? What, will you tear |
| | Impatient answers from my gentle tongue? |
| | Fie, fie! you counterfeit, you puppet, you! |

| | |
|---|---|
| **HERMIA** | 'Puppet'? Why so? Ay, that way goes the game. |
| | Now I perceive that she hath made compare 290 |
| | Between our statures; she hath urged her height; |
| | And with her personage, her tall personage, |
| | Her height, forsooth, she hath prevailed with him. |
| | And are you grown so high in his esteem |
| | Because I am so dwarfish and so low? 295 |
| | How low am I, thou painted maypole? Speak! |
| | How low am I? I am not yet so low |
| | But that my nails can reach unto thine eyes. |

| | |
|---|---|
| **HELENA** | I pray you, though you mock me, gentlemen, |
| | Let her not hurt me. I was never curst; 300 |
| | I have no gift at all in shrewishness. |
| | I am a right maid for my cowardice; |
| | Let her not strike me. You perhaps may think, |
| | Because she is something lower than myself, |
| | That I can match her. |

| | |
|---|---|
| **HERMIA** | Lower? Hark, again. 305 |

| | |
|---|---|
| **HELENA** | Good Hermia, do not be so bitter with me. |
| | I evermore did love you, Hermia, |
| | Did ever keep your counsels, never wronged you; |
| | Save that in love unto Demetrius |
| | I told him of your stealth unto this wood. 310 |
| | He followed you; for love I followed him; |
| | But he hath chid me hence, and threatened me |
| | To strike me, spurn me, nay, to kill me too. |
| | And now, so you will let me quiet go, |
| | To Athens will I bear my folly back, 315 |
| | And follow you no farther. Let me go. |
| | You see how simple and how fond I am. |

| | |
|---|---|
| **HERMIA** | Why, get you gone! Who is't that hinders you? |

| | |
|---|---|
| **HELENA** | A foolish heart that I leave here behind. |

| | |
|---|---|
| **HERMIA** | What! with Lysander? |

| | |
|---|---|
| **HELENA** | With Demetrius. 320 |

ORIGINAL

| | |
|---|---|
| **HELENA** | Stop! Have you no modesty, no female pride, no restraint? Do you want to yank retorts from my mouth? Shame on you, you two-faced dolly! |
| **HERMIA** | Dolly? Why do you call me that? Oh, so you want to call names! You ridicule me for being short? You boast of being taller? You won Lysander because you are taller than I. Have you grown in his admiration because I am lowly and shrunken? How low do you think I am, you painted flagpole? Tell me! How short am I by comparison? I am not too short to reach up and scratch your eyes out. |
| **HELENA** | Even though you men ridicule me, don't let Hermia hurt me. I am not scrappy. I am not good at arguing. Like a proper girl, I avoid fights. Don't let her hit me. You may think that, because she is shorter, I would win the fight. |
| **HERMIA** | Shorter? Again she makes fun of me. |
| **HELENA** | Hermia, don't be so bitter toward me. I always loved you, Hermia. I always kept your secrets and never harmed you. Except, I told Demetrius that you were eloping to the woods with Lysander. He followed you. Because I love him, I followed Demetrius. But he has scolded me, threatened to hit me, to reject me, even to kill me. Let me go quietly. I will return to Athens and follow you no more. Let me leave. You see how simple-minded and silly I am. |
| **HERMIA** | Then go! What stops you? |
| **HELENA** | A foolish heart that I leave here. |
| **HERMIA** | Do you leave it with Lysander? |
| **HELENA** | I leave it with Demetrius. |

ACT III

TRANSLATION

| | |
|---|---|
| **LYSANDER** | Be not afraid; she shall not harm thee, Helena. |
| **DEMETRIUS** | No, sir, she shall not, though you take her part. |

**HELENA**
O, when she's angry, she is keen and shrewd:
She was a vixen when she went to school;
And, though she be but little, she is fierce.                    325

**HERMIA**
'Little' again! Nothing but 'low' and 'little'!
Why will you suffer her to flout me thus?
Let me come to her.

**LYSANDER**                                   Get you gone, you dwarf,
You minimus of hind'ring knot-grass made,
You bead, you acorn.

**DEMETRIUS**                                  You are too officious                    330
In her behalf that scorns your services.
Let her alone: speak not of Helena,
Take not her part; for if thou dost intend
Never so little show of love to her,
Thou shalt aby it.

**LYSANDER**                                  Now she holds me not;                    335
Now follow, if thou dar'st, to try whose right,
Of thine or mine, is most in Helena.

**DEMETRIUS**
Follow? Nay, I'll go with thee, cheek by jowl.
*[Exeunt LYSANDER and DEMETRIUS]*

**HERMIA**
You, mistress, all this coil is 'long of you:
Nay, go not back.

**HELENA**                                   I will not trust you, I;                    340
Nor longer stay in your curst company.
Your hands than mine are quicker for a fray;
My legs are longer though, to run away.
*[Exit]*

**HERMIA**
I am amazed, and know not what to say.
*[Exit]*
*[OBERON and PUCK come forward]*

**OBERON**
This is thy negligence: still thou mistak'st,                    345
Or else committ'st thy knaveries willfully.

*i*

ORIGINAL

| | |
|---|---|
| **LYSANDER** | Don't worry. Hermia won't harm you, Helena. |
| **DEMETRIUS** | No, she won't, even though Lysander defends her. |
| **HELENA** | When Hermia's mad, she is sharp and shrewd. She was a schemer when she was in school. She may be short, but she's vicious. |
| **HERMIA** | You call me short! You keep calling me low and short! Why do you men let her insult me like this? Let me fight her. |
| **LYSANDER** | Go away, shortie. You tiny grass-eater, you bead, you acorn. |
| **DEMETRIUS** | You butt in and take the part of a woman who scorns you. Leave Hermia alone. Don't mention Helena's name. Don't defend her. If you don't love Hermia, you will pay for your intrusion. |
| **LYSANDER** | Hermia has no hold on me. Come fight me, if you dare, to see who deserves Helena. |
| **DEMETRIUS** | Follow you? No, I will accompany you, side by side. *[LYSANDER and DEMETRIUS depart.]* |
| **HERMIA** | All this arguing is your fault, Helena. Don't sneak away now. |
| **HELENA** | I don't trust you. I won't stay with you. You are more eager to fight than I am. My legs are longer than yours for running. *[HELENA departs.]* |
| **HERMIA** | I am stunned. I don't know what to say. *[HERMIA departs.]* *[OBERON and PUCK enter.]* |
| **OBERON** | Your carelessness caused this. You are always making errors, or else creating mischief. |

ACT III

TRANSLATION

PUCK          Believe me, King of Shadows, I mistook.
              Did not you tell me I should know the man
              By the Athenian garments he had on?
              And so far blameless proves my enterprise          350
              That I have 'nointed an Athenian's eyes:
              And so far am I glad it so did sort,
              As this their jangling I esteem a sport.

OBERON        Thou seest these lovers seek a place to fight:
              Hie therefore, Robin, overcast the night;           355
              The starry welkin cover thou anon
              With drooping fog as black as Acheron,
              And lead these testy rivals so astray
              As one come not within another's way.
              Like to Lysander sometime frame thy tongue,         360
              Then stir Demetrius up with bitter wrong,
              And sometime rail thou like Demetrius;
              And from each other look thou lead them thus,
              Till o'er their brows death-counterfeiting sleep
              With leaden legs and batty wings doth creep.        365
              Then crush this herb into Lysander's eye;
              Whose liquor hath this virtuous property,
              To take from thence all error with his might
              And make his eyeballs roll with wonted sight.
              When they next wake, all this derision              370
              Shall seem a dream and fruitless vision,
              And back to Athens shall the lovers wend
              With league whose date till death shall never end.
              Whiles I in this affair do thee employ,
              I'll to my queen, and beg her Indian boy;           375
              And then I will her charmed eye release
              From monster's view, and all things shall be peace.

PUCK          My fairy lord, this must be done with haste,
              For night's swift dragons cut the clouds full fast,
              And yonder shines Aurora's harbinger,               380
              At whose approach ghosts, wandering here and there,
              Troop home to churchyards. Damned spirits all,
              That in cross-ways and floods have burial,
              Already to their wormy beds are gone,
              For fear lest day should look their shames upon.     385
              They willfully exile themselves from light,
              And must for aye consort with black-browed night.

**PUCK**     Believe me, King of Shadows, it was a mistake. Didn't you tell me to look for a man in Athenian clothes? It wasn't my fault that I anointed the wrong Athenian. I'm glad I made a mistake. Their squabbling is fun.

**OBERON**     These men are looking for a place to fight. Hurry, Robin, and bring on darkness. Cover the sky in a fog as black as hell. Make Demetrius and Lysander lose their way and not encounter each other. Imitate Lysander's voice and anger Demetrius with a false accusation. Then do the same with Demetrius's voice. Keep confusing them until they fall asleep. Put magic pansy juice on Lysander's eyes. Use the magic to correct the error and make him see what he used to see. When they awaken, they will remember this squabbling as a dream. The lovers will return to Athens and never part. While you complete your assignment, I will return to Titania and beg for her servant boy. I will release her from the magic that makes her love Bottom. Everything will be peaceful again.

ACT III

**PUCK**     We must hurry, lord. Night is passing. It is almost dawn. It is time for ghosts to return to the cemetery. Doomed suicides buried at the crossroads and victims drowned at sea have returned to their coffins. Ghosts don't want to face their sins in daylight. They choose to hide from sunlight and to venture out only at night.

TRANSLATION

OBERON But we are spirits of another sort.
I with the morning's love have oft made sport;
And like a forester the groves may tread            390
Even till the eastern gate, all fiery-red,
Opening on Neptune with fair blessed beams,
Turns into yellow gold his salt-green streams.
But, notwithstanding, haste, make no delay:
We may effect this business yet ere day.            395
*[Exit]*

PUCK Up and down, up and down;
I will lead them up and down:
I am feared in field and town.
Goblin, lead them up and down.
Here comes one.                                      400
*[Enter LYSANDER]*

LYSANDER Where art thou, proud Demetrius? Speak thou now.

PUCK Here, villain, drawn and ready. Where art thou?

LYSANDER I will be with thee straight.

PUCK                                     Follow me, then,
To plainer ground.
*[Exit LYSANDER]*
*[Enter DEMETRIUS]*

DEMETRIUS                               Lysander! speak again.
Thou runaway, thou coward, art thou fled?            405
Speak! In some bush? Where dost thou hide thy head?

PUCK Thou coward, art thou bragging to the stars,
Telling the bushes that thou look'st for wars,
And wilt not come? Come, recreant, come, thou child,
I'll whip thee with a rod: he is defiled             410
That draws a sword on thee.

DEMETRIUS                               Yea, art thou there?

PUCK Follow my voice; we'll try no manhood here.
*[Exeunt]*
*[Enter LYSANDER]*

| | |
|---|---|
| **OBERON** | But we are a different kind of spirit. I love to frolic at dawn. Like a hunter, I walk the woods until morning. Until the green sea turns yellow with sunlight. But, hurry, don't dawdle. We may complete our task before daybreak. *[OBERON goes out.]* |
| **PUCK** | I will lead the men up and down the forest. People fear me in the country and in town. Elf, lead the men astray. Here comes one of them. *[LYSANDER enters.]* |
| **LYSANDER** | Where are you Demetrius? Answer me. |
| **PUCK** | Here, villain, with my sword held out. Where are you? |
| **LYSANDER** | I am coming straight toward you. |
| **PUCK** | Follow me to flatter ground. *[LYSANDER departs.]* *[DEMETRIUS enters.]* |
| **DEMETRIUS** | Lysander, answer me! Have you run away, you coward? Answer me! Are you lurking in the brush? Where are you hiding? |
| **PUCK** | You coward, are you bragging to heaven? Do you tell the underbrush that you intend to fight me? Why don't you approach me? Come on, playboy, come on, babyface. I will punish you with a stick. You dishonor anybody you fight with a man's sword. |
| **DEMETRIUS** | Where are you? |
| **PUCK** | Follow the sound of my voice. We can't fight here. *[PUCK and DEMETRIUS depart.]* *[LYSANDER enters.]* |

ACT III

TRANSLATION

| LYSANDER | He goes before me, and still dares me on; |
|---|---|

LYSANDER    He goes before me, and still dares me on;
When I come where he calls, then he is gone.
The villain is much lighter heeled than I;            415
I followed fast, but faster he did fly;
That fallen am I in dark uneven way,
And here will rest me. Come, thou gentle day!
*[Lies down]*
For if but once thou show me thy grey light,
I'll find Demetrius, and revenge this spite.          420
*[Sleeps]*
*[Enter PUCK and DEMETRIUS]*

PUCK    Ho, ho, ho! Coward, why com'st thou not?

DEMETRIUS    Abide me, if thou dar'st; for well I wot
Thou runn'st before me, shifting every place,
And dar'st not stand, nor look me in the face.
Where art thou now?

PUCK                          Come hither; I am here.          425

DEMETRIUS    Nay, then, thou mock'st me. Thou shalt buy this dear,
If ever I thy face by daylight see.
Now, go thy way. Faintness constraineth me
To measure out my length on this cold bed.
By day's approach look to be visited.                430
*[Sleeps]*
*[Enter HELENA]*

HELENA    O weary night, O long and tedious night,
Abate thy hours; shine comforts from the east,
That I may back to Athens by daylight,
From these that my poor company detest;
And sleep, that sometimes shuts up sorrow's eye,     435
Steal me awhile from mine own company.
*[Sleeps]*

PUCK    Yet but three? Come one more;
Two of both kinds makes up four.
Here she comes, curst and sad:
Cupid is a knavish lad,                               440
Thus to make poor females mad.
*[Enter HERMIA]*

| | |
|---|---|
| **LYSANDER** | Demetrius is in front of me and challenges me to fight. When I move closer to him, he has gone. The rascal is quicker on his feet than I. I followed him immediately, but he ran faster. I have fallen on rough ground. I will rest here until daylight! *[LYSANDER lies on the ground.]* As soon as dark night fades to gray, I'll locate Demetrius and beat him. *[LYSANDER falls asleep.]* *[PUCK and DEMETRIUS enter.]* |
| **PUCK** | Hey, coward, why have you stopped looking for me? |
| **DEMETRIUS** | Wait for me, if you dare. I know that you are really running from me. You shift around and refuse to stand still or to face me. Where are you now, Lysander? |
| **PUCK** | Come this way. I'm waiting for you. |
| **DEMETRIUS** | No you aren't. You are toying with me. You will pay for this trickery if I find you in daylight. Keep on running. I am so tired that I will lie on the ground. By daylight, I wIll find you. *[DEMETRIUS sleeps.]* *[HELENA enters.]* |
| **HELENA** | Oh, I wish this long, annoying night would end. I need daylight so I can return to Athens and escape these vicious people. I want to escape sadness by sleeping alone. *[HELENA falls asleep.]* |
| **PUCK** | There are only three here. I must wait for the fourth. Two males and two females adds up to four. Here comes Hermia, angry and sad. Cupid is a rascal to rile young women. *[HERMIA enters.]* |

ACT III

TRANSLATION

**HERMIA**       Never so weary, never so in woe,
Bedabbled with the dew, and torn with briers,
I can no further crawl, no further go.
My legs can keep no pace with my desires.    445
Here will I rest me till the break of day.
Heavens shield Lysander, if they mean a fray!
*[Sleeps]*

**PUCK**          On the ground
Sleep sound.
I'll apply    450
To your eye,
Gentle lover, remedy.
*[Squeezes the juice on LYSANDER's eyes]*
When thou wak'st,
Thou tak'st
True delight    455
In the sight
Of thy former lady's eye:
And the country proverb known,
That every man should take his own,
In your waking shall be shown:    460
Jack shall have Jill;
Nought shall go ill;
The man shall have his mare again, and all shall be well.
*[Exit PUCK]*

ORIGINAL

**HERMIA**     I am so weary of crawling through the dewy ground and thorns. I can go no further. My legs can't keep up with where I want to be. Let me rest here until daylight. God watch over Lysander if he intends to fight Demetrius! *[HERMIA sleeps.]*

**PUCK**     Sleep soundly on the ground. I will apply the magic pansy juice to your eyelid, Lysander. *[PUCK anoints LYSANDER's eyelids with the magic pansy juice.]* When you awaken, you will feel affection once more for Hermia. When you arise, you will prove the old saying that everyone belongs to his own love. Jack and Jill will come together. There will be no errors this time. Each man will have his mate once more and all will be well. *[PUCK goes out.]*

ACT III

TRANSLATION

# ACT IV, SCENE 1

## The woods near Athens.

*[Enter TITANIA, Queen of the Fairies, and BOTTOM, PEASEBLOSSOM, COBWEB,*
*MOTH, MUSTARDSEED, and other FAIRIES attending; OBERON behind, unseen]*

| | |
|---|---|
| **TITANIA** | Come, sit thee down upon this flowery bed, |
| | While I thy amiable cheeks do coy, |
| | And stick musk-roses in thy sleek smooth head, |
| | And kiss thy fair large ears, my gentle joy. |
| **BOTTOM** | Where's Peaseblossom? |
| **PEASEBLOSSOM** | Ready. |
| **BOTTOM** | Scratch my head, Peaseblossom. |
| | Where's Monsieur Cobweb? |
| **COBWEB** | Ready. |
| **BOTTOM** | Monsieur Cobweb; good monsieur, get you your |
| | weapons in your hand and kill me a red-hipped |
| | humble-bee on the top of a thistle; and, good |
| | monsieur, bring me the honey-bag. Do not fret |
| | yourself too much in the action, monsieur; and, |
| | good monsieur, have a care the honey-bag break |
| | not; I would be loath to have you overflown |
| | with a honey-bag, signior. Where's Monsieur |
| | Mustardseed? |
| **MUSTARDSEED** | Ready. |
| **BOTTOM** | Give me your neaf, Monsieur Mustardseed. |
| | Pray you, leave your curtesy, good monsieur. |
| **MUSTARDSEED** | What's your will? |

Line numbers: 5, 10, 15, 20

# ACT IV, SCENE 1

The woods outside the Greek city-state of Athens.

*[TITANIA, Queen of the Fairies, enters with BOTTOM, PEASEBLOSSOM, COBWEB, MOTH, MUSTARDSEED, and the fairy attendants. OBERON lurks behind out of sight.]*

| | |
|---|---|
| **TITANIA** | Come here, Bottom, and sit on this flower bed while I caress your sweet cheeks. I will place musk roses in your hair, and kiss your long ears, my sweet delight. |
| **BOTTOM** | Where's Peaseblossom? |
| **PEASEBLOSSOM** | I'm ready. |
| **BOTTOM** | Scratch my head, Peaseblossom. Where's Mr. Spiderweb? |
| **COBWEB** | I'm ready. |
| **BOTTOM** | Mr. Spiderweb, sir, draw your weapons. Kill a red-bottomed bumblebee sitting on a thistle. Dear sir, bring me the honey bag. Don't waste time, sir. And, good sir, don't rupture the honey bag. Sir, I would hate to have you soaked in honey. Where's Mr. Mustardseed? |
| **MUSTARDSEED** | I'm ready. |
| **BOTTOM** | Hold out your fist, Mr. Mustardseed. Please, don't stand there stiffly, sir. |
| **MUSTARDSEED** | What do you want? |

ACT IV

TRANSLATION

BOTTOM    Nothing, good monsieur, but to help Cavalery
          Cobweb to scratch. I must to the barber's, monsieur;
          for methinks I am marvellous hairy about          25
          the face; and I am such a tender ass, if my hair
          do but tickle me I must scratch.

TITANIA   What, wilt thou hear some music, my sweet love?

BOTTOM    I have a reasonable good ear in music; let
          us have the tongs and the bones.                  30

TITANIA   Or say, sweet love, what thou desir'st to eat.

BOTTOM    Truly, a peck of provender; I could munch your
          good dry oats. Methinks I have a great desire to
          a bottle of hay: good hay, sweet hay, hath no
          fellow.                                            35

TITANIA   I have a venturous fairy that shall seek
          The squirrel's hoard, and fetch thee new nuts.

BOTTOM    I had rather have a handful or two of dried peas.
          But, I pray you, let none of your people stir me;
          I have an exposition of sleep come upon me.       40

TITANIA   Sleep thou, and I will wind thee in my arms.
          Fairies, be gone, and be all ways away.
          *[Exeunt FAIRIES]*
          So doth the woodbine the sweet honeysuckle
          Gently entwist, the female ivy so
          Enrings the barky fingers of the elm.             45
          O, how I love thee! How I dote on thee!
          *[They sleep]*
          *[OBERON advances; Enter PUCK]*

| | |
|---|---|
| BOTTOM | Only to help Sir Spiderweb scratch me. Sir, I must go to a barber. I seem to have a terribly furry face. I am such a tender donkey that tickling hairs make me itch. |
| TITANIA | Would you like music, sweetheart? |
| BOTTOM | I am an appreciator of music. Let's hear rattling tongs and bone clappers. |
| TITANIA | Tell me, sweetheart, what you want to eat. |
| BOTTOM | Indeed, a bag of horse feed. I would like to munch dry oats. I would also enjoy a bale of hay. There's nothing like good, sweet hay. |
| TITANIA | I have a venturesome fairy who will get new nuts from the squirrel's hoard. |
| BOTTOM | I would rather have some handfuls of dried peas. Please, let no fairies disturb me. I feel sleepy. |
| TITANIA | Sleep while I hold you in my arms. Fairies, go away and stay away. *[The FAIRIES go out.]* Just as vines intertwine honeysuckle. Just as ivy climbs around elm bark. Oh, how I love you! How I adore you! *[TITANIA and BOTTOM fall asleep.] [OBERON enters. PUCK arrives.]* |

ACT IV

OBERON

Welcome, good Robin. Seest thou this sweet sight?
Her dotage now I do begin to pity;
For, meeting her of late behind the wood
Seeking sweet favours for this hateful fool,                    50
I did upbraid her and fall out with her,
For she his hairy temples then had rounded
With coronet of fresh and fragrant flowers;
And that same dew, which sometime on the buds
Was wont to swell like round and orient pearls,                 55
Stood now within the pretty flow'rets' eyes,
Like tears that did their own disgrace bewail.
When I had at my pleasure taunted her,
And she in mild terms begged my patience,
I then did ask of her her changeling child,                     60
Which straight she gave me, and her fairy sent
To bear him to my bower in fairy land.
And now I have the boy, I will undo
This hateful imperfection of her eyes.
And, gentle Puck, take this transformed scalp                   65
From off the head of this Athenian swain,
That he awaking when the other do,
May all to Athens back again repair,
And think no more of this night's accidents
But as the fierce vexation of a dream.                          70
But first I will release the fairy queen.
*[He drops the juice on TITANIA's eyelids]*
Be as thou wast wont to be;
See as thou was wont to see.
Dian's bud o'er Cupid's flower
Hath such force and blessed power.                              75
Now, my Titania; wake you, my sweet queen.

TITANIA

*[Waking]* My Oberon! what visions have I seen!
Methought I was enamoured of an ass.

OBERON

There lies your love.

TITANIA

How came these things to pass?                                 80
O, how mine eyes do loathe his visage now!

OBERON

Silence awhile. Robin, take off this head.
Titania, music call, and strike more dead
Than common sleep of all these five the sense.

**OBERON**   Welcome, Robin. Do you see this sweet pair? I suspect Titania is senile. When I saw her flirting in the woods with this wretched simpleton, I scolded her and argued with her. She placed a crown of fresh-picked, sweet flowers on his furry head. The dew that sometimes stands like Asian pearls on blossoms stood now on the flower centers like tears mourning their humiliation. I enjoyed teasing her. She sweetly asked me to indulge her. I asked for her Indian servant boy. She immediately gave him to me. She sent her fairy to carry the child to my quarters in fairy land. Now that the boy is mine, I will correct her infatuation with Bottom. Puck, remove the ass's head from this Athenian man. When he arises with the other players, may everything in Athens return to normal. May everyone think of last night's misadventures as a wicked nightmare. First, I will take the magic spell away from Titania. *[OBERON anoints TITANIA's eyelids with magic pansy juice.]* Return to normal. See clearly again. The blossom of the blue-flowered chaste tree is the antidote to the purple pansy. Now, my Titania, arise, dear queen.

ACT IV

**TITANIA**   *[Arising]* Oberon, what a bad dream I had! I thought I fell in love with a donkey.

**OBERON**   There he lies.

**TITANIA**   How did this happen? He is horrible to look at!

**OBERON**   Be still, please. Robin, remove the donkey's head from Bottom. Titania, call for music to wake up Bottom and the four Athenian lovers.

| | |
|---|---|
| TITANIA | Music, ho! music; such as charmeth sleep. 85 |
| | *[Still music]* |
| PUCK | Now when thou wak'st, with thine own fool's eyes peep. |
| OBERON | Sound, music! |
| | *[The music changes]* |
| | Come, my queen, take hands with me, |
| | And rock the ground whereon these sleepers be. |
| | *[They dance]* |
| | Now thou and I are new in amity, 90 |
| | And will to-morrow midnight solemnly |
| | Dance in Duke Theseus' house triumphantly, |
| | And bless it to all fair prosperity. |
| | There shall the pairs of faithful lovers be |
| | Wedded, with Theseus, all in jollity. 95 |
| PUCK | Fairy king, attend and mark: |
| | I do hear the morning lark. |
| OBERON | Then, my queen, in silence sad, |
| | Trip we after night's shade. |
| | We the globe can compass soon, 100 |
| | Swifter than the wand'ring moon. |
| TITANIA | Come, my lord; and in our flight, |
| | Tell me how it came this night |
| | That I sleeping here was found |
| | With these mortals on the ground. 105 |
| | *[Exeunt OBERON, TITANIA, and PUCK;* |
| | *Wind horns within; Enter THESEUS,* |
| | *HIPPOLYTA, EGEUS, and Train]* |
| THESEUS | Go, one of you, find out the forester; |
| | For now our observation is performed; |
| | And since we have the vaward of the day, |
| | My love shall hear the music of my hounds, |
| | Uncouple in the western valley; go: 110 |
| | Dispatch, I say, and find the forester. |
| | *[Exit an ATTENDANT]* |
| | We will, fair queen, up to the mountain's top, |
| | And mark the musical confusion |
| | Of hounds and echo in conjunction. |

ORIGINAL

| | |
|---|---|
| **TITANIA** | Play music that lulls people to sleep. *[Quiet music.]* |
| **PUCK** | When you all arise, look out with your usual stupid eyes. |
| **OBERON** | Loud music! *[The music grows louder.]* Come, Titania, take my hands and stamp the ground where the sleepers lie. *[OBERON and TITANIA dance.]* You and I are lovers again. We will dance tomorrow midnight at Duke Theseus's palace and bless the household with fertility. There, these two pairs of lovers will marry and join Theseus in wedding celebration. |
| **PUCK** | Oberon, King of the Fairies, listen. The lark announces the morning. |
| **OBERON** | Then, Titania, in serious quiet, let's follow the night. Let's fly around the world faster than the moon can travel. |
| **TITANIA** | Come, Oberon, and on the way, tell me what happened tonight. Why did I sleep on the ground near these humans? *[OBERON, TITANIA, and PUCK fly away. Hunting horns sound. THESEUS, HIPPOLYTA, EGEUS, and their company enter.]* |
| **THESEUS** | Someone go locate the hunter now that we have celebrated Midsummer's Eve. Because it is still early, Hippolyta shall hear the baying of my hunting dogs unleashed in the western valley. Go, hurry, I say. Locate the hunter. *[A servant goes out.]* We will climb the mountain, Titania, and listen to the music of dogs baying and the echo of their cries. |

ACT IV

TRANSLATION

| | |
|---|---|
| **HIPPOLYTA** | I was with Hercules and Cadmus once      115 |
| | When in a wood of Crete they bayed the bear |
| | With hounds of Sparta: never did I hear |
| | Such gallant chiding; for, besides the groves, |
| | The skies, the fountains, every region near |
| | Seemed all one mutual cry: I never heard      120 |
| | So musical a discord, such sweet thunder. |
| | |
| **THESEUS** | My hounds are bred out of the Spartan kind, |
| | So flewed, so sanded; and their heads are hung |
| | With ears that sweep away the morning dew; |
| | Crook-knee'd and dew-lapped like Thessalian bulls;      125 |
| | Slow in pursuit, but matched in mouth like bells, |
| | Each under each. A cry more tuneable |
| | Was never hollow'd to, nor cheered with horn, |
| | In Crete, in Sparta, nor in Thessaly. |
| | Judge when you hear. But, soft, what nymphs are these?      130 |
| | |
| **EGEUS** | My lord, this is my daughter here asleep; |
| | And this Lysander; this Demetrius is; |
| | This Helena, old Nedar's Helena: |
| | I wonder of their being here together. |
| | |
| **THESEUS** | No doubt they rose up early to observe      135 |
| | The rite of May; and, hearing our intent, |
| | Came here in grace of our solemnity. |
| | But speak, Egeus; is not this the day |
| | That Hermia should give answer of her choice? |
| | |
| **EGEUS** | It is, my lord.      140 |
| | |
| **THESEUS** | Go, bid the huntsmen wake them with their horns. |
| | *[Horns, and shout within; DEMETRIUS,* |
| | *LYSANDER, HERMIA, and HELENA awake* |
| | *and start up]* |
| | Good-morrow, friends. Saint Valentine is past; |
| | Begin these wood-birds but to couple now? |
| | |
| **LYSANDER** | Pardon, my lord. |
| | *[He and the rest kneel to THESEUS]* |
| | |
| **THESEUS** | I pray you all, stand up.      145 |
| | I know you two are rival enemies; |
| | How comes this gentle concord in the world, |
| | That hatred is so far from jealousy |
| | To sleep by hate, and fear no enmity? |

ORIGINAL

| | |
|---|---|
| **HIPPOLYTA** | I accompanied Hercules and Cadmus once in the forests of Crete when Spartan hounds chased a bear. I never heard such gorgeous dog voices. The woods, sky, springs, and every direction sounded one call. I never heard so melodic a variety, like sweet thunder. |
| **THESEUS** | My hunting dogs are a Spartan breed, with the same sandy-colored bloodhound mouths. They have the same ears that drag the grass. They are bowlegged and droopy-throated like Greek bulls. They are slow runners, but their cries sound like harmonized bells. There is no cry so melodious to the calls of hunters and the blare of horns in Crete, Sparta, or Thessaly. Listen for yourself. Look, what young girls are lying here? |
| **EGEUS** | Duke Theseus, this is my daughter Hermia sleeping here. This man is Lysander and this one, Demetrius. This girl is Helena, Nedar's daughter. I wonder why the four of them sleep here together. |
| **THESEUS** | They probably got up early to celebrate May Day. They may have learned of our plans and came to honor our morning ceremony. Tell me, Egeus, is this the day that Hermia was going to accept or reject Demetrius? |
| **EGEUS** | It is, my lord. |
| **THESEUS** | Go, have the hunters sound their horns. *[A shout and the hunters' horns emerge from the woods. DEMETRIUS, LYSANDER, HERMIA, and HELENA arise.]* Good morning, all. It is long past Saint Valentine's Day. Are you lovebirds choosing your mates today? |
| **LYSANDER** | Pardon, my lord. *[LYSANDER and the others kneel before Duke THESEUS.]* |
| **THESEUS** | Please, arise, all of you. I know Demetrius and Lysander are rivals for Hermia. Why are you all at peace this morning? How have you slept here together without arousing anger? |

ACT IV

TRANSLATION

LYSANDER       My lord, I shall reply amazedly,                                    150
               Half 'sleep, half waking; but as yet, I swear,
               I cannot truly say how I came here.
               But, as I think—for truly would I speak,
               And now I do bethink me, so it is—
               I came with Hermia hither. Our intent                               155
               Was to be gone from Athens, where we might,
               Without the peril of the Athenian law—

EGEUS          Enough, enough, my lord; you have enough.
               I beg the law, the law upon his head.
               They would have stol'n away, they would, Demetrius,                 160
               Thereby to have defeated you and me:
               You of your wife, and me of my consent,
               Of my consent that she should be your wife.

DEMETRIUS      My lord, fair Helen told me of their stealth,
               Of this their purpose hither to this wood;                          165
               And I in fury hither followed them,
               Fair Helena in fancy following me.
               But, my good lord, I wot not by what power
               (But by some power it is) my love to Hermia,
               Melted as the snow seems to me now                                  170
               As the remembrance of an idle gaud
               Which in my childhood I did dote upon:
               And all the faith, the virtue of my heart,
               The object and the pleasure of mine eye,
               Is only Helena. To her, my lord,                                    175
               Was I betrothed ere I saw Hermia:
               But like a sickness did I loathe this food;
               But, as in health, come to my natural taste,
               Now I do wish it, love it, long for it,
               And will for evermore be true to it.                                180

THESEUS        Fair lovers, you are fortunately met:
               Of this discourse we more will hear anon.
               Egeus, I will overbear your will;
               For in the temple, by and by with us,
               These couples shall eternally be knit.                              185
               And, for the morning now is something worn,
               Our purposed hunting shall be set aside.
               Away with us to Athens, three and three,
               We'll hold a feast in great solemnity.
               Come, Hippolyta.                                                    190
               *[Exeunt THESEUS, HIPPOLYTA, EGEUS, and Train]*

ORIGINAL

**LYSANDER**  Although I am only half awake, I admit to being surprised. I don't know how I arrived here. As I recall, Hermia and I came here together. We wanted to escape Athenian law by eloping.

**EGEUS**  Stop him, my lord. You have heard enough. I beg you decide against Lysander for breaking the law. He and Hermia eloped. They intended to outwit me and Demetrius. You would lose your future wife. I would lose my right to choose a husband for Hermia.

**DEMETRIUS**  Theseus, Helena told me about the elopement to the woods. I pursued them in anger. Helena followed me. Lord, some power caused me to stop loving Hermia. I gave her up like a toy left over from my boyhood. Truly, I want only Helena. I was engaged to Helena before I met Hermia. As though sick, I rejected Helena. I am cured. I want only Helena forever to love and be loyal to.

**ACT IV**

**THESEUS**  Young couples, it is fortunate that you gathered here. I will listen to your situation soon. Egeus, I overrule your power over your daughter. In the temples, these four will be married at my wedding to Hippolyta. Since it is late morning, I will leave our hunt. Come join us in Athens, three grooms and three brides, to share our wedding feast. Come, Hippolyta. *[THESEUS, HIPPOLYTA, EGEUS, and their company depart.]*

TRANSLATION

| | |
|---|---|
| **DEMETRIUS** | These things seem small and undistinguishable, |
| | Like far-off mountains turned into clouds. |
| **HERMIA** | Methinks I see these things with parted eye, |
| | When every thing seems double. |
| **HELENA** | So methinks: |
| | And I have found Demetrius like a jewel. 195 |
| | Mine own, and not mine own. |
| **DEMETRIUS** | It seems to me |
| | That yet we sleep, we dream. Do not you think |
| | The Duke was here, and bid us follow him? |
| **HERMIA** | Yea, and my father. |
| **HELENA** | And Hippolyta. 200 |
| **LYSANDER** | And he did bid us follow to the temple. |
| **DEMETRIUS** | Why, then, we are awake: let's follow him; |
| | And by the way let us recount our dreams. |
| | *[Exeunt]* |
| | *[BOTTOM wakes]* |
| **BOTTOM** | When my cue comes, call me, and I will answer. |
| | My next is 'Most fair Pyramus.' Heigh-ho! Peter 205 |
| | Quince! Flute, the bellows-mender! Snout, the |
| | tinker! Starveling! God's my life, stol'n hence, |
| | and left me asleep! I have had a most rare vision. |
| | I have had a dream past the wit of man to say |
| | what dream it was. Man is but an ass if he go 210 |
| | about to expound this dream. Methought I was— |
| | there is no man can tell what. Methought I was, |
| | and methought I had—but man is but a patched |
| | fool if he will offer to say what me thought I had. |
| | The eye of man hath not heard, the ear of man 215 |
| | hath not seen; man's hand is not able to taste, his |
| | tongue to conceive, nor his heart to report, what my |
| | dream was. I will get Peter Quince to write a ballad |
| | of this dream: it shall be called 'Bottom's Dream,' |
| | because it hath no bottom; and I will sing it in the 220 |
| | latter end of a play, before the Duke. Peradventure, |
| | to make it the more gracious, I shall sing it at her death. |
| | *[Exit]* |

| | |
|---|---|
| **DEMETRIUS** | These events seem tiny and indistinct, like cloud-covered mountains in the distance. |
| **HERMIA** | I recall events out of focus, as though I were seeing double. |
| **HELENA** | Me, too. I have located Demetrius like a lost gem. He is mine, but like something recovered. |
| **DEMETRIUS** | We seem to be still asleep and dreaming. Did Duke Theseus really appear and invite us to the palace? |
| **HERMIA** | Yes, he came with my father. |
| **HELENA** | And with Hippolyta. |
| **LYSANDER** | He invited us to the temple. |
| **DEMETRIUS** | Then we are awake. Let's follow him. Along the way, let's share our dreams. [*The four depart toward Athens.*] [*BOTTOM wakes up.*] |
| **BOTTOM** | When my cue is next, call me and I will play my part. The next cue is "Handsome Pyramus." Hey! Peter Quince! Flute, the bellows repairman! Snout, the tin repairer! Starveling! God save me, they have crept away and left me sleeping. I have had a strange nightmare. I have had an unexplainable dream. It is stupid to interpret such a dream. I thought I was—no one could say what. I thought I was, I thought I had—but man is only a clown if he says what I had. No eye has heard, no ear has seen, no hand can taste, no tongue can imagine, no heart can say what I dreamed. I will have Peter Quince write a ballad about my nightmare. It will be entitled "Bottom's Dream," because it was endless. At the end of the play, I will sing it for Duke Theseus. To make it more elegant, I will sing it at Thisby's death. [*BOTTOM departs.*] |

ACT IV

TRANSLATION

# ACT IV, SCENE 2

## Athens. A room in Quince's house.

*[Enter QUINCE, FLUTE, SNOUT, and STARVELING]*

QUINCE            Have you sent to Bottom's house? Is he come
                  home yet?

STARVELING        He cannot be heard of. Out of doubt, he is transported.

FLUTE             If he come not, then the play is marred; it goes
                  Not forward, doth it?                                        5

QUINCE            It is not possible: you have not a man in all
                  Athens able to discharge Pyramus but he.

FLUTE             No; he hath simply the best wit of any handicraft
                  man in Athens.

QUINCE            Yea, and the best person too: and he is a very            10
                  Paramour for a sweet voice.

FLUTE             You must say paragon: a paramour is, God
                  bless us, a thing of naught.
                  *[Enter SNUG the joiner]*

SNUG              Masters, the Duke is coming from the temple;
                  and there is two or three lords and ladies more          15
                  married. If our sport had gone forward, we had
                  all been made men.

FLUTE             O sweet bully Bottom! Thus hath he lost six-
                  pence a day during his life. He could not have
                  'scaped sixpence a-day; and the Duke had not             20
                  given him sixpence a-day for playing Pyramus,
                  I'll be hanged; he would have deserved it: six-
                  pence a-day in Pyramus, or nothing.
                  *[Enter BOTTOM]*

BOTTOM            Where are these lads? Where are these hearts?

QUINCE            Bottom! O most courageous day! O most happy hour!        25

BOTTOM            Masters, I am to discourse wonders: but ask me
                  Not what; for if I tell you, I am not true Athenian.
                  I will tell you everything, right as it fell out.

QUINCE            Let us hear, sweet Bottom.

# ACT IV, SCENE 2

In a room of QUINCE's house in Athens, a Greek city-state.

*[QUINCE, FLUTE, SNOUT, and STARVELING enter.]*

| | |
|---|---|
| **QUINCE** | Did you send someone to Bottom's house? Has he arrived home yet? |
| **STARVELING** | No one knows where he is. Surely, he has been kidnapped. |
| **FLUTE** | If he doesn't arrive, the play is ruined. We can't perform, can we? |
| **QUINCE** | It is impossible. Nobody in Athens can take Bottom's place in the role of Pyramus. |
| **FLUTE** | I agree. Bottom is the wittiest Athenian laborer. |
| **QUINCE** | Yes, and he's the best man, too. He has the voice of a lover. |
| **FLUTE** | You mean the voice of a model. A lover is, God knows, wicked. *[SNUG the furniture maker enters.]* |
| **SNUG** | Workers, Duke Theseus is coming from the temple. There are two or three more couples wed. If we had performed our play, we might have become citizens. |
| **FLUTE** | Oh dear old pal, Bottom! He has lost a pension of six pennies a day. He would surely have earned six pennies a day. I will be hanged if the Duke would not have allotted Bottom six pennies a day for life for playing the role of Pyramus. Bottom would have earned it. No less than six pennies a day for Pyramus. *[BOTTOM enters.]* |
| **BOTTOM** | Where are the players? Where are these fellows? |
| **QUINCE** | Bottom! Oh uplifting day! Oh lucky day! |
| **BOTTOM** | Workers, I have stories to tell you, but don't ask me about them. If I tell you the truth, I am not a true Athenian. I will tell you everything, just as it happened. |
| **QUINCE** | We're listening, Bottom. |

ACT IV

TRANSLATION

**BOTTOM**     Not a word of me. All that I will tell you is,                          30
that the Duke hath dined. Get your apparel together;
good strings to your beards, new ribbons to your
pumps; meet presently at the palace; every man look
over his part. For the short and the long is, our play is
preferred. In any case, let Thisby have clean linen; and        35
let not him that plays the lion pare his nails, for they
shall hang out for the lion's claws. And, most dear
actors, eat no onions nor garlick, for we are to
utter sweet breath; and I do not doubt but to
hear them say it is a sweet comedy. No more                     40
words. Away, go, away!
*[Exeunt]*

ORIGINAL

BOTTOM

I won't say a word. All I can tell you is that Duke Theseus has finished dinner. Get your costumes together. Put strong strings on your fake beards and new ribbons in your shoes. Let's meet at the palace. Every player study his part. In conclusion, it is time to perform. And finally, let Thisby have clean underwear. Let the lion player not trim his nails. For they will hang down like lion's claws. And, dear players, eat no onions or garlic, for we should have pleasing breath. The audience will say it is a sweet comedy. No more talking. Hurry, hurry! *[They depart.]*

ACT IV

# ACT V, SCENE 1

## Athens. The palace of Theseus.

*[Enter THESEUS, HIPPOLYTA, PHILOSTRATE, Lords and Attendants]*

**HIPPOLYTA**     'Tis strange, my Theseus, that these lovers speak of.

**THESEUS**     More strange than true. I never may believe
These antique fables, nor these fairy toys.
Lovers and madmen have such seething brains,
Such shaping fantasies, that apprehend                    5
More than cool reason ever comprehends.
The lunatic, the lover, and the poet
Are of imagination all compact:
One sees more devils than vast hell can hold;
That is the madman. The lover, all as frantic,          10
Sees Helen's beauty in a brow of Egypt.
The poet's eye, in a fine frenzy rolling,
Doth glance from heaven to earth, from earth to heaven;
And as imagination bodies forth
The forms of things unknown, the poet's pen             15
Turns them to shapes, and gives to airy nothing
A local habitation and a name.
Such tricks hath strong imagination,
That, if it would but apprehend some joy,
It comprehends some bringer of that joy;                20
Or in the night, imagining some fear,
How easy is a bush supposed a bear?

**HIPPOLYTA**     But all the story of the night told over,
And all their minds transfigured so together,
More witnesseth than fancy's images,                    25
And grows to something of great constancy;
But, howsoever, strange and admirable.
*[Enter LYSANDER, DEMETRIUS, HERMIA,
and HELENA]*

# ACT V, SCENE 1

The palace of Duke Theseus in Athens, a Greek city-state.

*[THESEUS, HIPPOLYTA, PHILOSTRATE, lords, and servants enter.]*

**HIPPOLYTA**     It is strange, Theseus, the stories these lovers tell.

**THESEUS**     Too strange to be true. I never believe ancient fables or fairy tales. Lovers and madmen have such confused brains, such fantasies. They see more than sanity can accept. The madman, lover, and poet think alike. One imagines more demons than hell can contain. That is the lunatic. The lover, who is just as frenzied, sees the beauty of Helen of Troy in an Egyptian face. The poet, looking wildly about, glances from sky to earth and back up again. As imagination dictates, the poet describes fantasies. He turns mere nothings into local places and people. Such deception requires a vivid fancy. If the imagination sees a delight, it makes up a reason to be happy. Also, at night, the imagination can transform a bush into a fearful bear.

**HIPPOLYTA**     They told their whole story of last night. Together, they produced a tale of transformation. Four witnesses were consistent in their accounts of fanciful events. But, the story was strange and wonderful. *[LYSANDER, DEMETRIUS, HERMIA, and HELENA enter.]*

TRANSLATION

THESEUS          Here come the lovers, full of joy and mirth.
Joy, gentle friends! Joy and fresh days of love
Accompany your hearts!

LYSANDER                    More than to us    30
Wait in your royal walks, your board, your bed!

THESEUS          Come now; what masques, what dances shall we have,
To wear away this long age of three hours
Between our after-supper and bed-time?
Where is our usual manager of mirth?    35
What revels are in hand? Is there no play
To ease the anguish of a torturing hour?
Call Philostrate.

PHILOSTRATE             Here, mighty Theseus.

THESEUS          Say, what abridgment have you for this evening?
What masque? What music? How shall we beguile    40
The lazy time, if not with some delight?

PHILOSTRATE     There is a brief how many sports are ripe;
Make choice of which your highness will see first.
*[Giving a paper]*

THESEUS          *[Reads]* 'The battle with the Centaurs, to be sung
By an Athenian eunuch to the harp.'    45
We'll none of that; that have I told my love,
In glory of my kinsman Hercules.
'The riot of the tipsy Bacchanals,
Tearing the Thracian singer in their rage.'
That is an old device, and it was played    50
When I from Thebes came last a conqueror.
'The thrice three Muses mourning for the death
Of learning, late deceased in beggary.'
That is some satire, keen and critical,
Not sorting with a nuptial ceremony.    55
'A tedious brief scene of young Pyramus
And his love Thisby; very tragical mirth.'
Merry and tragical? Tedious and brief?
That is hot ice and wondrous strange black snow.
How shall we find the concord of this discord?    60

| | |
|---|---|
| **THESEUS** | Here come the four lovers, happy and laughing. Joy to you, friends! Joy and more loving days fill your hearts! |
| **LYSANDER** | We anticipate even more happiness in your palace path, your table, your lovemaking! |
| **THESEUS** | Join us. What scenes, what dances shall we watch to use up the three hours between the banquet and bedtime? Where is Philostrate, the master of amusement? What entertainment have you planned? Is there a performance to hurry the time? Summon Philostrate. |
| **PHILOSTRATE** | Here I am, mighty Theseus. |
| **THESEUS** | Tell me, what pastime have you scheduled for tonight? What scene? What music? How shall we endure these slow hours if not with some fun? |
| **PHILOSTRATE** | Here is a list of amusements ready for you. Choose what you want to see first. *[PHILOSTRATE hands THESEUS the list of amusements.]* |
| **THESEUS** | *[THESEUS reads aloud.]* A castrated Athenian male playing the harp and singing "The Battle with the Centaurs." We don't want that one. I have already told Hippolyta about the exploits of my cousin Hercules. "The riot of the drunken Bacchanals, murdering Orpheus the singer." This has been overdone. I last heard it when I returned victorious from Thebes. "The three muses mourning the death of scholarship, which died a pauper." That is a satire, harsh and mocking, not suited for a wedding celebration. "An annoying short scene of young Pyramus and his lover Thisby, a tragic bit of fun." Fun and tragic? Annoying and short? This sounds odd, like hot ice and black snow. How will we understand this confusion? |

ACT V

| | |
|---|---|
| **PHILOSTRATE** | A play there is, my lord, some ten words long, |
| | Which is as 'brief' as I have known a play; |
| | But by ten words, my lord, it is too long, |
| | Which makes it 'tedious'. For in all the play |
| | There is not one word apt, one player fitted. |
| | And 'tragical', my noble lord, it is, |
| | For Pyramus therein doth kill himself; |
| | Which when I saw rehearsed, I must confess, |
| | Made mine eyes water; but more 'merry' tears |
| | The passion of loud laughter never shed. |

65

70

| | |
|---|---|
| **THESEUS** | What are they that do play it? |

| | |
|---|---|
| **PHILOSTRATE** | Hard-handed men that work in Athens here, |
| | Which never laboured in their minds till now; |
| | And now have toiled their unbreathed memories |
| | With this same play against your nuptial. |

75

| | |
|---|---|
| **THESEUS** | And we will hear it. |

| | |
|---|---|
| **PHILOSTRATE** | No, my noble lord, |
| | It is not for you: I have heard it over, |
| | And it is nothing, nothing in the world, |
| | Unless you can find sport in their intents, |
| | Extremely stretched, and conned with cruel pain, |
| | To do you service. |

80

| | |
|---|---|
| **THESEUS** | I will hear that play; |
| | For never anything can be amiss |
| | When simpleness and duty tender it. |
| | Go, bring them in: and take your places, ladies. |
| | *[Exit PHILOSTRATE]* |

| | |
|---|---|
| **HIPPOLYTA** | I love not to see wretchedness o'er-charged, |
| | And duty in his service perishing. |

85

| | |
|---|---|
| **THESEUS** | Why, gentle sweet, you shall see no such thing. |

| | |
|---|---|
| **HIPPOLYTA** | He says they can do nothing in this kind. |

ORIGINAL

**PHILOSTRATE**   The play is only ten words long. It is the briefest play I have ever seen. But even ten words is too long. Even short, the play is annoying. The play is all nonsense. The players are unsuited to the stage. It is tragic because Pyramus commits suicide. Truly, I shed tears when I watched the rehearsal. But the tears were from laughing out loud.

**THESEUS**   Who are the actors?

**PHILOSTRATE**   They are Athenian laborers who have never used their brains until now. They have strained their unused brains to perform this play for your wedding.

**THESEUS**   We will hear it.

**PHILOSTRATE**   No, my lord, you won't like it. I have heard it all. It is worthless. Unless you plan to laugh at their efforts to stretch the myth and to memorize their lines to honor you.

**THESEUS**   I will hear their play. Nothing so simple-minded and sincere can be wrong. Bring in the players. Ladies, be seated. *[PHILOSTRATE goes out.]*

**HIPPOLYTA**   I don't like to see workers pressed beyond their abilities. Or honor to the Duke destroying itself.

**THESEUS**   Sweetheart, don't worry.

**HIPPOLYTA**   Philostrate says they are harmless.

ACT V

| | |
|---|---|
| **THESEUS** | The kinder we, to give them thanks for nothing. |
| | Our sport shall be to take what they mistake;      90 |
| | And what poor duty cannot do, |
| | Noble respect takes it in might, not merit. |
| | Where I have come, great clerks have purposed |
| | To greet me with premeditated welcomes, |
| | Where I have seen them shiver and look pale,      95 |
| | Make periods in the midst of sentences, |
| | Throttle their practised accent in their fears, |
| | And, in conclusion, dumbly have broke off, |
| | Not paying me a welcome. Trust me, sweet, |
| | Out of this silence yet I picked a welcome;      100 |
| | And in the modesty of fearful duty |
| | I read as much as from the rattling tongue |
| | Of saucy and audacious eloquence. |
| | Love, therefore, and tongue-tied simplicity |
| | In least speak most to my capacity.      105 |
| | *[Enter PHILOSTRATE]* |
| **PHILOSTRATE** | So please your grace, the Prologue is addressed. |
| **THESEUS** | Let him approach. |
| | *[Flourish of trumpets; Enter QUINCE, as PROLOGUE]* |
| **QUINCE** | *(as Prologue)* 'If we offend, it is with our good will. |
| | That you should think, we come not to offend, |
| | But with good will. To show our simple skill,      110 |
| | That is the true beginning of our end. |
| | Consider then, we come but in despite. |
| | We do not come, as minding to content you, |
| | Our true intent is. All for your delight |
| | We are not here. That you should here repent you,      115 |
| | The actors are at hand: and, by their show, |
| | You shall know all that you are like to know,' |
| **THESEUS** | This fellow doth not stand upon points. |
| **LYSANDER** | He hath rid his prologue like a rough colt; he |
| | Knows not the stop. A good moral, my lord: it      120 |
| | is not enough to speak, but to speak true. |
| **HIPPOLYTA** | Indeed he hath played on this prologue like a |
| | Child on a recorder; a sound, but not in government. |

| | |
|---|---|
| **THESEUS** | We will be kind to the players and thank them for their efforts. We will laugh at their errors. What they do poorly, we will respect rather than judge. In the past, I have encountered court officials trying to honor me with long speeches. I have seen them tremble, turn pale, pause in the middle, and choke on their words out of fear. In the end, they stopped welcoming me. Even in their failure, sweetheart, I have found welcome. I admire their shyness at a fearful job more than I admire grand eloquence. Their admiration and fumbling ignorance won me over. *[PHILOSTRATE enters.]* |
| **PHILOSTRATE** | If you are ready, Duke Theseus, the introducer is ready. |
| **THESEUS** | Let him enter. *[A trumpet fanfare sounds. QUINCE, the introducer, enters.]* |
| **QUINCE** | *(QUINCE playing the role of the introducer)* If we insult you, we mean well. Don't think we deliberately insult you. We come out of goodwill. To show our humble skill, that is our purpose. Look at it this way, we come but to defy you. We didn't come intending to please you. We are not here to delight you. If you regret listening to the play, the actors are ready. And by their performance, you will learn all you can know about the play. |
| **THESEUS** | This man makes no sense. |
| **LYSANDER** | He rides his speech like a jolting horse. He doesn't stop at the ends of sentences. Here is a lesson, Duke Theseus: One must speak and be true to the meaning. |
| **HIPPOLYTA** | He plays the introduction like a small child on a flute. He makes sounds, but no melody. |

ACT V

| | |
|---|---|
| **THESEUS** | His speech was like a tangled chain; nothing |
| | impaired, but all disordered. Who is next? 125 |
| | *[Enter with a Trumpeter before them* |
| | *BOTTOM as PYRAMUS, FLUTE as THISBY,* |
| | *SNOUT as WALL, STARVELING as MOONSHINE,* |
| | *and SNUG as LION]* |
| | |
| **QUINCE** | *(as Prologue)* Gentles, perchance you wonder at this show; |
| | But wonder on, till truth make all things plain. |
| | This man is Pyramus, if you would know; |
| | This beauteous lady Thisby is, certain. |
| | This man, with lime and rough-cast, doth present 130 |
| | Wall, that vile Wall which did these lovers sunder; |
| | And through Wall's chink, poor souls, they are content |
| | To whisper, at the which let no man wonder. |
| | This man, with lanthorn, dog, and bush of thorn, |
| | Presenteth Moonshine; for, if you will know, 135 |
| | By moonshine did these lovers think no scorn |
| | To meet at Ninus' tomb, there, there to woo. |
| | This grisly beast, which Lion hight by name, |
| | The trusty Thisby, coming first by night, |
| | Did scare away, or rather did affright; 140 |
| | And as she fled, her mantle she did fall, |
| | Which Lion vile with bloody mouth did stain. |
| | Anon comes Pyramus, sweet youth, and tall, |
| | And finds his trusty Thisby's mantle slain; |
| | Whereat with blade, with bloody blameful blade, 145 |
| | He bravely broached his boiling bloody breast; |
| | And Thisby, tarrying in mulberry shade, |
| | His dagger drew, and died. For all the rest, |
| | Let Lion, Moonshine, Wall, and lovers twain, |
| | At large discourse while here they do remain. 150 |
| | *[Exeunt QUINCE, BOTTOM, FLUTE,* |
| | *SNUG, and STARVELING]* |
| | |
| **THESEUS** | I wonder if the lion be to speak. |
| | |
| **DEMETRIUS** | No wonder, my lord: one lion may, when many |
| | asses do. |

| | |
|---|---|
| **THESEUS** | His speech is like a tangled chain. It isn't broken, but it's nonsense. Which actor speaks next? *[A trumpeter leads in BOTTOM as Pyramus, FLUTE as Thisby, SNOUT as Wall, STARVELING as Moonlight, and SNUG as the lion.]* |
| **QUINCE** | *(QUINCE playing the role of the introducer)* Gentlefolk, you may wonder at this play. Keep on listening until everything is clear to you. This player is Pyramus. This beautiful lady is Thisby. This player, covered in lime and concrete, signifies a wall, which keeps Pyramus and Thisby apart. Through the gap, the poor lovers whisper to each other. This player, with lantern, dog, and thorn-bush, represents moonlight because Pyramus and Thisby met to court by moonlight at Ninus's grave. This fierce beast, called Lion, Thisby scared away earlier in the night. As she ran, her cloak fell. The lion stained it with his bloody jaws. Pyramus soon arrives and finds his loving Thisby's stained cloak. With his dagger, he stabbed himself in the chest. Thisby, waiting under a mulberry tree, took his dagger and killed herself. For the rest of the story, listen to Lion, Moonlight, Wall, and the two lovers. *[QUINCE, BOTTOM, FLUTE, SNUG, and STARVELING depart.]* |
| **THESEUS** | I wonder if the lion has a speaking part. |
| **DEMETRIUS** | Why not, my lord. A lion should speak, just like many asses. |

TRANSLATION

| | |
|---|---|
| SNOUT | *(as Wall)* In this same interlude it doth befall |
| | That I, one Snout by name, present a wall; 155 |
| | And such a wall as I would have you think |
| | That had in it a crannied hole or chink, |
| | Through which the lovers, Pyramus and Thisby, |
| | Did whisper often, very secretly. |
| | This loam, this rough-cast, and this stone, doth show 160 |
| | That I am that same wall; the truth is so. |
| | And this the cranny is, right and sinister, |
| | Through which the fearful lovers are to whisper. |
| THESEUS | Would you desire lime and hair to speak better? |
| DEMETRIUS | It is the wittiest partition that ever I heard discourse, 165 |
| | my lord. |
| | *[Enter BOTTOM as PYRAMUS]* |
| THESEUS | Pyramus draws near the wall; silence. |
| BOTTOM | *(as Pyramus)* O grim-looked night! O night with hue |
| | so black! O night, which ever art when day is not! |
| | O night, O night, alack, alack, alack, 170 |
| | I fear my Thisby's promise is forgot! |
| | And thou, O wall, O sweet, O lovely wall, |
| | That stand'st between her father's ground and mine; |
| | Thou wall, O wall, O sweet and lovely wall, |
| | Show me thy chink, to blink through with mine eyne. 175 |
| | *[WALL holds up his fingers]* |
| | Thanks, courteous wall: Jove shield thee well for this! |
| | But what see I? No Thisby do I see. |
| | O wicked wall, through whom I see no bliss, |
| | Cursed be thy stones for thus deceiving me! |
| THESEUS | The wall, methinks, being sensible, should curse again. 180 |
| BOTTOM | *(as Pyramus)* No, in truth, sir, he should not. 'Deceiving |
| | me' is Thisby's cue; she is to enter now, and I am to |
| | spy her through the wall. You shall see it will |
| | fall pat as I told you. Yonder she comes. |
| | *[Enter THISBY]* |
| FLUTE | *(as Thisby)* O wall, full often hast thou heard my moans, 185 |
| | For parting my fair Pyramus and me: |
| | My cherry lips have often kissed thy stones: |
| | Thy stones with lime and hair knit up in thee. |

ORIGINAL

SNOUT

*(SNOUT playing the role of Wall)* In this plot, I, Snout the actor, play a wall. In this wall there was a hole or gap. Through the gap, Pyramus and Thisby whispered in secret. This dirt, this concrete, these pebbles prove that I am the wall. This is true. And this gap, right to left, is where the lovers whisper.

THESEUS

Do you need lime and hair to be a better wall?

DEMETRIUS

That is the funniest wall I ever heard speak, my lord. *[BOTTOM appears in the role of Pyramus.]*

THESEUS

Pyramus is approaching the wall. Silence.

BOTTOM

*(BOTTOM playing the role of Pyramus)* Oh, grim night! Oh, black-colored night! Oh, night, which can never be day! Oh night, night, woe, woe, woe, I am afraid that Thisby has forgotten me! Oh, dear, beautiful Wall, you stand between her father's property and mine. And you, Wall, sweet, dear Wall, show me the gap that I can look through. *[Wall holds up two fingers in a V.]* Thanks, courteous Wall. Jupiter protect you for this gap! What do I see? I see no Thisby. Oh evil Wall, through which I see no happiness, I curse your stones for tricking me.

THESEUS

The Wall should curse him back.

BOTTOM

*(BOTTOM playing the role of Pyramus)* No, truly, sir, the wall should not speak now. "Deceiving me" is Thisby's cue. She will enter now. I will spy on her through the gap in the wall. You will see it all work out as I said. Here comes Thisby. *[Thisby enters.]*

FLUTE

*(FLUTE playing the role of Thisby)* Oh, Wall, you have often heard me moan at this separation between me and Pyramus. My red lips have often kissed your stones. These stones cemented with lime and hair in the mortar.

ACT V

TRANSLATION

| | |
|---|---|
| **BOTTOM** | *(as Pyramus)* I see a voice; now will I to the chink, |
| | To spy an I can hear my Thisby's face.     190 |
| | Thisby! |
| **FLUTE** | *(as Thisby)* My love! Thou art my love, I think. |
| **BOTTOM** | *(as Pyramus)* Think what thou wilt, I am thy lover's grace; |
| | And like Limander am I trusty still. |
| **FLUTE** | *(as Thisby)* And I like Helen, till the fates me kill.     195 |
| **BOTTOM** | *(as Pyramus)* Not Shafalus to Procrus was so true. |
| **FLUTE** | *(as Thisby)* As Shafalus to Procrus, I to you. |
| **BOTTOM** | *(as Pyramus)* O, kiss me through the hole of this vile wall. |
| **FLUTE** | *(as Thisby)* I kiss the wall's hole, not your lips at all. |
| **BOTTOM** | *(as Pyramus)* Wilt thou at Ninny's tomb meet me     200 |
| | straightway? |
| **FLUTE** | *(as Thisby)* Tide life, tide death, I come without delay. |
| | *[Exeunt BOTTOM and FLUTE]* |
| **SNOUT** | *(as Wall)* Thus have I, Wall, my part discharged so; |
| | And, being done, thus Wall away doth go. |
| | *[Exit]* |
| **THESEUS** | Now is the mural down between the two neighbours.     205 |
| **DEMETRIUS** | No remedy, my lord, when walls are so wilful to |
| | Hear without warning. |
| **HIPPOLYTA** | This is the silliest stuff that ever I heard. |
| **THESEUS** | The best in this kind are but shadows; and the |
| | worst are no worse, if imagination amend them.     210 |

| BOTTOM | *(BOTTOM playing the role of Pyramus)* I see a voice. I will go to the gap to spy and hear Thisby's face. Thisby! |
|---|---|
| FLUTE | *(FLUTE playing the role of Thisby)* My love. I think you are my love. |
| BOTTOM | *(BOTTOM playing the role of Pyramus)* Think what you wish, I am your lover. And like Leander, who swam the Hellespont each night to visit his sweetheart Hero, I am faithful. |
| FLUTE | *(FLUTE playing the role of Thisby)* And I, like Hero, Leander's love, am faithful until death. |
| BOTTOM | *(BOTTOM playing the role of Pyramus)* Even Cephalus was never so faithful to his sweetheart Procris as I am to you. |
| FLUTE | *(FLUTE playing the role of Thisby)* As Cephalus was to Procris, so am I faithful to you. |
| BOTTOM | *(BOTTOM playing the role of Pyramus)* Oh, kiss me through the gap in this wall. |
| FLUTE | *(FLUTE playing the role of Thisby)* I can't reach through the gap to your lips. |
| BOTTOM | *(BOTTOM playing the role of Pyramus)* Will you meet me now at Ninus's grave? |
| FLUTE | *(FLUTE playing the role of Thisby)* Come life or death, I will meet you immediately. *[BOTTOM and FLUTE depart separately.]* |
| SNOUT | *(SNOUT playing the role of Wall)* I, in the part of Wall, have finished my lines. And, because I'm finished, Wall will depart the stage. *[SNOUT goes out.]* |
| THESEUS | The wall between the two neighbors is down. |
| DEMETRIUS | There is no cure for walls that eavesdrop without warning the whisperers. |
| HIPPOLYTA | This is the silliest play I ever saw. |
| THESEUS | Plays are only actors pretending to be people. Even the worst are good if the audience has imagination. |

ACT V

| | |
|---|---|
| **HIPPOLYTA** | It must be your imagination then, and not theirs. |
| **THESEUS** | If we imagine no worse of them than they<br>of themselves, they may pass for excellent men.<br>*[Enter SNUG as LION and STARVELING as MOONSHINE]*<br>Here come two noble beasts in, a moon and a lion. |
| **SNUG** | *(as Lion)* You, ladies, you, whose gentle hearts do fear    215<br>The smallest monstrous mouse that creeps on floor,<br>May now, perchance, both quake and tremble here,<br>When lion rough in wildest rage doth roar.<br>Then know that I, one Snug the joiner, am<br>A lion fell, nor else no lion's dam:    220<br>For, if I should as lion come in strife<br>Into this place, 'twere pity on my life. |
| **THESEUS** | A very gentle beast, and of a good conscience. |
| **DEMETRIUS** | The very best at a beast, my lord, that e'er I saw. |
| **LYSANDER** | This lion is a very fox for his valour.    225 |
| **THESEUS** | True; and a goose for his discretion. |
| **DEMETRIUS** | Not so, my lord; for his valour cannot carry his<br>discretion, and the fox carries the goose. |
| **THESEUS** | His discretion, I am sure, cannot carry his valour;<br>for the goose carries not the fox. It is well;    230<br>leave it to his discretion, and let us listen to the moon. |
| **STARVELING** | *(as Moonshine)* This lanthorn doth the horned moon<br>present— |
| **DEMETRIUS** | He should have worn the horns on his head. |
| **THESEUS** | He is no crescent, and his horns are invisible    235<br>Within the circumference. |
| **STARVELING** | *(as Moonshine)* This lanthorn doth the horned moon present;<br>Myself the man i' the moon do seem to be. |
| **THESEUS** | This is the greatest error of all the rest: the man<br>should be put into the lantern. How is it else    240<br>the man i' the moon? |
| **DEMETRIUS** | He dares not come there for the candle: for, you<br>see, it is already in snuff. |

ORIGINAL

| | |
|---|---|
| **HIPPOLYTA** | It must be the fantasy of the audience and not the actors' imagination. |
| **THESEUS** | If we assume that there can be no worse acting troupe than this, these actors are superb. *[SNUG in the role of the lion and STARVELING playing Moonlight enter the stage.]* Here come two more grand creatures, a moon and a lion. |
| **SNUG** | *(SNUG playing the role of Lion)* Ladies, I know you fear the tiniest mouse-monster that creeps over the floor. You may shake and quiver when this stage lion roars. Please understand that I, Snug the furniture maker, am a dangerous lion, not a lioness. If something attacks me in the role, I will die. |
| **THESEUS** | A mild-mannered creature with a conscience. |
| **DEMETRIUS** | The best creature I ever saw. |
| **LYSANDER** | This lion is foxier than he is brave. |
| **THESEUS** | Yes, he is. And he's a nitwit for telling us. |
| **DEMETRIUS** | You're wrong, my lord. His bravery does not outweigh his caution. Thus, the fox carries off the goose. |
| **THESEUS** | His caution certainly can't outweigh his courage. For a goose can't carry off a fox. It doesn't matter. Let his caution be enough. Let's hear the moon. |
| **STARVELING** | *(STARVELING playing the role of Moonlight)* This lantern represents the sharp ends of the crescent moon. |
| **DEMETRIUS** | He should wear the sharp ends on his head. |
| **THESEUS** | He is no new moon. The sharp ends are not visible without the rest of the round moon. |
| **STARVELING** | *(STARVELING playing the role of Moonlight)* This lantern represents the sharp ends of the moon. I am playing the role of the man in the moon. |
| **THESEUS** | This is the worst error in the play. They should stuff the actor inside the lantern. That's the only way he can be the man in the moon. |
| **DEMETRIUS** | There is room for a candle, but not the man. Look. The candle is already insulted. |

**ACT V**

TRANSLATION

| | |
|---|---|
| HIPPOLYTA | I am aweary of this moon: would he would change! |
| THESEUS | It appears, by his small light of discretion, that      245<br>he is in the wane: but yet, in courtesy, in all reason,<br>we must stay the time. |
| LYSANDER | Proceed, moon. |
| STARVELING | *(as Moonshine)* All that I have to say, is to tell you<br>that the lanthorn is the moon; I, the man i' the moon; this    250<br>thornbush, my thornbush; and this dog, my dog. |
| DEMETRIUS | Why, all these should be in the lantern; for all<br>these are in the moon. But silence; here comes Thisby.<br>*[Enter FLUTE as THISBY]* |
| FLUTE | *(as Thisby)* This is old Ninny's tomb. Where is my love? |
| SNUG | *(as Lion)* Oh!      255<br>*[LION roars; THISBY runs off]* |
| DEMETRIUS | Well roared, lion. |
| THESEUS | Well run, Thisby. |
| HIPPOLYTA | Well shone, moon. Truly, the moon shines with a good grace.<br>*[LION worries THISBY's Mantle, and exits]* |
| THESEUS | Well moused, lion. |
| DEMETRIUS | And so comes Pyramus.      260 |
| LYSANDER | And then the lion vanishes.<br>*[Enter BOTTOM as PYRAMUS]* |
| BOTTOM | *(as Pyramus)* Sweet moon, I thank thee for thy sunny beams;<br>I thank thee, moon, for shining now so bright:<br>For, by thy gracious golden, glittering gleams,<br>I trust to take of truest Thisby's sight.      265<br>But stay—O spite!<br>But mark, poor knight,<br>What dreadful dole is here!<br>Eyes, do you see?<br>How can it be?      270<br>O dainty duck! O dear!<br>Thy mantle good,<br>What! stained with blood?<br>Approach, ye furies fell!<br>O fates! come, come,      275<br>Cut thread and thrum,<br>Quail, rush, conclude, and quell! |

ORIGINAL

| | |
|---|---|
| **HIPPOLYTA** | I am bored with this moon. I wish he would change into something else! |
| **THESEUS** | It seems that so small a light represents the shrinking moon. To be polite, we have to stay for the whole play. |
| **LYSANDER** | Say your part, moon. |
| **STARVELING** | *(STARVELING playing the role of Moonlight)* All I need to say is that the lantern represents the moon. And I represent the man in the moon. This thornbush is my thornbush. This dog is my dog. |
| **DEMETRIUS** | All these items should be inside the lantern. They are what we see on the moon. Hush. Here comes Thisby. *[FLUTE enters the stage playing the role of Thisby.]* |
| **FLUTE** | *(FLUTE playing the role of Thisby)* This is Ninus's grave. Where is Pyramus? |
| **SNUG** | *(SNUG playing the role of Lion)* Oh! *[When the lion roars, Thisby runs from the stage.]* |
| **DEMETRIUS** | Lion, you roared well. |
| **THESEUS** | Thisby, you ran well. |
| **HIPPOLYTA** | Moon, you shone well. Indeed, the moon shines generously. *[The lion paws over Thisby's cloak, then leaves the stage.]* |
| **THESEUS** | Lion, you trampled the cloak as though it were a mouse. |
| **DEMETRIUS** | Here comes Pyramus. |
| **LYSANDER** | And the lion will depart. *[BOTTOM comes on stage playing the part of Pyramus.]* |
| **BOTTOM** | *(BOTTOM playing the role of Pyramus)* Sweet moon, thanks for your sunshine. I thank you for glowing brightly. I thank you for generous gold and glittering rays. I will get a good view of Thisby. Wait—oh evil sight! Poor Pyramus, what sadness lies ahead! Eyes, do you see it? How did this happen? My dainty duck! Oh dear Thisby! Is this your cloak soaked with blood? Come down, dangerous goddesses of bad luck! Oh destiny! Come and snip the thread of life. Crush, hurry, end, and kill me! |

ACT V

TRANSLATION

| | |
|---|---|
| **THESEUS** | This passion, and the death of a dear friend, would go near to make a man look sad. |
| **HIPPOLYTA** | Beshrew my heart, but I pity the man. 280 |
| **BOTTOM** | *(as Pyramus)* O wherefore, nature, didst thou lions frame? Since lion vile hath here deflowered my dear; Which is—no, no—which was the fairest dame That lived, that loved, that liked, that looked with cheer. Come, tears, confound; 285 Out, sword, and wound The pap of Pyramus: Ay, that left pap, Where heart doth hop: Thus die I, thus, thus, thus. 290 *[He stabs himself]* Now am I dead, Now am I fled; My soul is in the sky: Tongue, lose thy light! Moon, take thy flight! 295 *[Exit STARVELING]* Now die, die, die, die, die. *[He dies]* |
| **DEMETRIUS** | No die, but an ace, for him; for he is but one. |
| **LYSANDER** | Less than an ace, man; for he is dead; he is nothing. |
| **THESEUS** | With the help of a surgeon he might yet recover and prove an ass. 300 |
| **HIPPOLYTA** | How chance moonshine is gone before Thisby comes back and finds her lover? |
| **THESEUS** | She will find him by starlight. Here she comes; And her passion ends the play. *[Enter FLUTE as THISBY]* |
| **HIPPOLYTA** | Methinks she should not use a long one for such 305 a Pyramus; I hope she will be brief. |
| **DEMETRIUS** | A mote will turn the balance, which Pyramus, Which Thisby, is the better: he for a man, God warrant us; she for a woman, God bless us. |

ORIGINAL

| | |
|---|---|
| **THESEUS** | All this emotion and the death of a dear friend would make anybody sad. |
| **HIPPOLYTA** | Forgive me. I pity Pyramus. |
| **BOTTOM** | *(BOTTOM playing the role of Pyramus)* Why did nature make lions? This lion has killed my sweetheart. Who is—no—who was the prettiest woman that lived, loved, enjoyed, and smiled. Come, my tears, and destroy me. My sword, strike Pyramus in the nipple. Hit the left nipple, under which my heart beats. And so I die like this and this and this. *[Pyramus stabs himself.]* I am dead and my spirit has flown away. My soul is in the sky. Words, see no more! Moon, fly away! *[STARVELING playing the role of Moonlight departs from the stage.]* Now I die, die, die, die, die. *[Pyramus collapses.]* |
| **DEMETRIUS** | He earns no dice, but an ace. He gets only one point. |
| **LYSANDER** | He earns less than one point. He is dead. He has no value. |
| **THESEUS** | With the aid of a physician, Pyramus might recover and be even sillier. |
| **HIPPOLYTA** | Why did Moonlight leave the stage before Thisby appears to discover Pyramus's death? |
| **THESEUS** | She will have to see by starlight. Here she comes. The play ends with her grief. *[FLUTE comes onstage in the role of Thisby.]* |
| **HIPPOLYTA** | She shouldn't say much about Pyramus. I hope Thisby's speech is short. |
| **DEMETRIUS** | A speck of dust determines who is the better actor, Pyramus or Thisby. He as a man. She as a woman. |

**ACT V**

TRANSLATION

| | | |
|---|---|---|
| **LYSANDER** | She hath spied him already with those sweet eyes. | 310 |
| **DEMETRIUS** | And thus she means, videlicet— | |
| **FLUTE** | *(as Thisby)* Asleep, my love? | |
| | What, dead, my dove? | |
| | O Pyramus, arise, | |
| | Speak, speak. Quite dumb? | 315 |
| | Dead, dead? A tomb | |
| | Must cover thy sweet eyes. | |
| | These lily lips, | |
| | This cherry nose, | |
| | These yellow cowslip cheeks, | 320 |
| | Are gone, are gone: | |
| | Lovers, make moan! | |
| | His eyes were green as leeks. | |
| | O Sisters Three, | |
| | Come, come to me, | 325 |
| | With hands as pale as milk; | |
| | Lay them in gore, | |
| | Since you have shore | |
| | With shears his thread of silk. | |
| | Tongue, not a word: | 330 |
| | Come, trusty sword; | |
| | Come, blade, my breast imbrue; | |
| | *[Stabs herself]* | |
| | And farewell, friends: | |
| | Thus Thisby ends; | |
| | Adieu, adieu, adieu. | 335 |
| | *[Dies]* | |
| **THESEUS** | Moonshine and Lion are left to bury the dead. | |
| **DEMETRIUS** | Ay, and Wall too. | |
| **BOTTOM** | No, I assure you; the wall is down that parted | |
| | their fathers. Will it please you to see the epilogue, | |
| | or to hear a Bergomask dance between | 340 |
| | two of our company? | |
| | *[BOTTOM and FLUTE stand up]* | |

| LYSANDER | Her dear eyes have already seen the corpse. |
|---|---|
| DEMETRIUS | Next comes her mourning. |

**FLUTE** *(FLUTE playing the role of Thisby)* Are you asleep, Pyramus? Can you be dead, my dove? Oh, Pyramus, get up. Speak to me. Are you forever silent? Are you dead? A grave will cover your eyes. Your white lips, your cherry-red nose, your flower-yellow cheeks, gone forever. Lovers, mourn with me! His eyes were green like onions. Oh, Fates, hold out white hands to me. Place them in blood. You have cut his silken thread of life. My mouth says nothing. Here, faithful sword. Come to my chest and stain it red with blood. *[Thisby stabs herself.]* Goodbye, friends. Thisby's life is ended. Goodbye, goodbye, goodbye. *[Thisby dies.]*

**THESEUS** Only Moonlight and Lion remain to bury Pyramus and Thisby.

**DEMETRIUS** Don't forget Wall.

**BOTTOM** No, I am certain that the wall between neighbors is gone. Would you like to see a closing speech? Would you rather hear an Italian dance performed by two of the actors? *[BOTTOM and FLUTE stand before the Duke.]*

ACT V

TRANSLATION

THESEUS       No epilogue, I pray you; for your play needs no
excuse. Never excuse; for when the players are
all dead there need none to be blamed. Marry,
if he that writ it had played Pyramus, and     345
hanged himself in Thisby's garter, it would have
been a fine tragedy: and so it is, truly; and very
notably discharged. But come, your Bergo-
mask; let your epilogue alone.
*[The company return; then two of them dance; then*
*BOTTOM, FLUTE, and their fellows exit]*
The iron tongue of midnight hath told twelve:     350
Lovers, to bed; 'tis almost fairy time.
I fear we shall out-sleep the coming morn,
As much as we this night have overwatched.
This palpable-gross play hath well beguiled
The heavy gait of night. Sweet friends, to bed.     355
A fortnight hold we this solemnity,
In nightly revels and new jollity.
*[Exeunt]*
*[Enter PUCK carrying a broom]*

PUCK          Now the hungry lion roars,
And the wolf behowls the moon;
Whilst the heavy ploughman snores,     360
All with weary task fordone.
Now the wasted brands do glow,
Whilst the scritch-owl, scritching loud,
Puts the wretch that lies in woe
In remembrance of a shroud.     365
Now it is the time of night
That the graves, all gaping wide,
Every one lets forth its sprite,
In the church-way paths to glide:
And we fairies, that do run     370
By the triple Hecate's team
From the presence of the sun,
Following darkness like a dream,
Now are frolic; not a mouse
Shall disturb this hallowed house:     375
I am sent with broom before,
To sweep the dust behind the door.
*[Enter OBERON and TITANIA, with all their Train]*

ORIGINAL

**THESEUS**     No closing speech, please. There is no excuse for this play.
Never explain the outcome. After the characters die, no
one deserves blame. If the playwright had taken the role
of Pyramus and made a noose of Thisby's garter to hang
himself, it would have been a better tragedy. A good
tragedy well acted. Perform the Italian dance. Forget
the closing speech. *[After the actors return to the stage,
two players dance. Then BOTTOM, FLUTE, and the rest
depart.]* I heard a bell strike 12:00 midnight. Newlyweds,
go to bed. It is time for fairies to frolic. I suspect we will
oversleep to make up for staying up so late. This idiotic
play has amused us tonight. Friends, go to bed. We will
celebrate every night for two weeks. *[They depart.]*
*[PUCK comes in with a broom.]*

**PUCK**        It is the time of night when lions roar and wolves howl
at the moon. The farmer snores after a hard day of
plowing. Dying torches burn down to embers. The owl,
screeching loud, causes the mourner to think of burial
garments. It is the time of night when ghosts climb out
of open graves. Spirits wander the cemetery. Fairies that
accompany the witch Hecate flee sunlight and enjoy the
night. Not even a mouse will disturb the palace. I carry
a broom for sweeping dust from behind the door.
*[OBERON, TITANIA, and their company enter.]*

ACT V

TRANSLATION

**OBERON**  Through the house give glimmering light,
By the dead and drowsy fire:
Every elf and fairy sprite                           380
Hop as light as bird from briar,
And this ditty, after me,
Sing and dance it trippingly.

**TITANIA**  First, rehearse your song by rote,
To each word a warbling note;                        385
Hand in hand, with fairy grace,
Will we sing, and bless this place.
*[Song and dance]*

**OBERON**  Now, until the break of day,
Through this house each fairy stray,
To the best bride-bed will we,                       390
Which by us shall blessed be;
And the issue there create
Ever shall be fortunate.
So shall all the couples three
Ever true in loving be;                              395
And the blots of Nature's hand
Shall not in their issue stand:
Never mole, hare-lip, nor scar,
Nor mark prodigious, such as are
Despised in nativity,                               400
Shall upon their children be.
With this field-dew consecrate,
Every fairy take his gait,
And each several chamber bless
Through this palace, with sweet peace;              405
E'er shall it in safety rest,
And the owner of it blest.
Trip away:
Make no stay:
Meet me all by break of day.                        410
*[Exeunt all but PUCK]*

ORIGINAL

**OBERON**  Spread light through the palace near the dying fire. Every elf and fairy must hop like a bird from a branch. And sing and dance to my song.

**TITANIA**  Teach them the song by singing the notes and saying the words. Holding hands, we fairies will sing and bless the palace. *[The FAIRIES sing and dance.]*

**OBERON**  Until dawn, fairies, wander the palace. Sanctify each couple's bed so their children will have good luck. Make the three marriages last forever. Let no birth defects harm their babies. Let no mole, deformed mouth, scar, or birthmark touch their children. Bless the marriages with dewdrops. Each fairy walk through the bedrooms and give the sleepers peace. Let the newlyweds be safe and blessed. Go on your way. Don't linger. Meet me at dawn. *[Everyone except PUCK leaves the stage.]*

ACT V

TRANSLATION

PUCK          If we shadows have offended,
Think but this, and all is mended,
That you have but slumbered here
While these visions did appear.
And this weak and idle theme,          415
No more yielding but a dream,
Gentles, do not reprehend;
If you pardon, we will mend.
And, as I am an honest Puck,
If we have unearned luck          420
Now to 'scape the serpent's tongue,
We will make amends ere long;
Else the Puck a liar call:
So, good night unto you all.
Give me your hands, if we be friends,          425
And Robin shall restore amends.
*[Exit]*

ORIGINAL

PUCK      If the actors have offended you, take comfort. You have
          been dreaming here and watching visions. Think of the
          play as a blameless dream. If you allow us, we will do
          better next time. I say sincerely, if we avoid hisses, we will
          perform a better play soon. Or else, Puck tells lies.
          Goodnight to the audience. Applaud if you feel friendly.
          Robin Goodfellow will correct all wrongs. *[PUCK goes
          out.]*

ACT V

TRANSLATION

# Questions for Reflection

1. Compare and contrast Demetrius and Lysander as potential husbands for Hermia. Why do Egeus and the Duke prefer Demetrius? Which youth is more influenced by money and which by love? Why does Demetrius deserve a scolding from Theseus?

2. Consider the details of the elopement. Why does the plan take into consideration the factors of distance, law, money, a doting widowed aunt, a short period of time, woods, and darkness?

3. Cite lines from *A Midsummer Night's Dream* that stress the physical differences between Hermia and Helena. How would you comment on Shakespeare's belief that true love does not arise from the admiration of blonde hair or long limbs?

4. Compare and contrast the romantic experiences of the following female characters from the play and from myth:

   - Procris
   - Hermia
   - Titania
   - Hippolyta
   - Helena
   - Hero
   - Thisby
   - Diana
   - Dido
   - Vestals
   - Daphne
   - Philomel
   - Aurora
   - Venus
   - nuns
   - a widowed aunt

   What themes does Shakespeare extract from these lives? How does the tragic story of Orpheus differ?

5. Describe Oberon's relationships with Titania, Puck, the Indian servant boy, the royal couple, Bottom, and Demetrius. What idiosyncrasies does Oberon share with Egeus and the Duke? Why are magic and invisibility useful to Oberon?

6. How does Shakespeare use nature lore in the play? What is the significance of the following: a roaring lion, a lark, a nightingale, a snake shedding its skin, a black beetle, the new moon, and seasons? How does Shakespeare enhance Theseus's importance to Athens by having the players meet under the Duke's oak?

7. Write an extended definition of malapropism using examples from speeches delivered by Quince (as Prologue), Pyramus, and Thisby. How does mixed imagery reflect on muddled lovers and unseasonable weather?

8. In regards to jealousy, what do mutual accusations of disloyalty suggest about the behaviors of Oberon and Titania? Which accusations seem more believable? more damning? more forgivable?

9. Consider the chaos that consumes the countryside when the seasons are no longer predictable. What is Shakespeare's view of metaphysical powers that meddle with human life, nature, and prosperity?

10. What is the importance of storytelling to the plot? How does Titania humanize her Indian boy with memories of his mother and pleasant days by the seaside watching sailboats? How do sails symbolize pregnancy and blessing?

11. Why does Helena assume that Lysander, Demetrius, and Hermia conspire to mock her? How has Demetrius betrayed her before the play begins? Why does she risk a second courtship with a fickle youth?

12. Consider the harsh laws allowing an Athenian father to condemn to death a disobedient daughter. How does Theseus display more compassion for Hermia than the girl's own father? Why does the play omit reference to Hermia's mother? Why does the stereotypical contrast of city and country take on more serious meaning in the play?

13. How is Lysander a better choice of husband for Hermia than Demetrius? Summarize Lysander's attitude toward troubled romances? How does he behave before and after the triple wedding?

14. Predict the strengths and weaknesses of the three marriages. Which wife is most likely to demand equality? to feel happily mated? to be truly loved? to make a worthy parent?

15. What is the value of this play to the celebration of a royal or aristocratic wedding? How could a sixteenth-century director incorporate music, costume, dance, lighting, backdrop, and spectacle to enhance a magical atmosphere?

16. What qualities are exhibited by the following characters?

   - Robin Starveling
   - Tom Snout
   - Peaseblossom
   - Cobweb
   - Nick Bottom
   - Peter Quince
   - Robin Goodfellow
   - Mustardseed
   - Moth
   - Francis Flute
   - Snug
   - Indian priestess

   What characteristics do they share or lack—particularly in terms of confidence, daring, obedience, balance, sympathy, and self-control? Which character is most rebellious? most egotistical? humblest? most loyal? least predictable? most easily flattered? most pompous? Why do you think that Shakespeare stresses character faults in a play about courtship, transformation, and marriage?

17. What is the importance of May Day and the maypole to the seasonal celebrations of peasants? How does the annual holiday compare with Valentine's Day in its influence on courtship?

18. Explain the theme of illusion versus reality as it applies to Bottom, Helena, Titania, Puck, Lysander, Demetrius, and Hermia. Why does Oberon pity Titania? How does his behavior change in the remainder of the play?

19. Justify the use of magic juices from a purple pansy and the chaste plant to realign loving relationships. Why are elements such as midsummer and the supernatural appropriate to a court masque? Why does the play conclude on the night of the new moon?

20. "What is an anti-masque and how does *A Midsummer Night's Dream* exhibit anti-masque characteristics? How does the tragic outcome of "Pyramus and Thisby" balance the triple wedding at the temple? How does the vot'ress's death in childbirth contrast the blessings of fairies throughout the palace bedrooms?

21. Summarize the tone of the "Lord, what fools these mortals be" speech. How does Shakespeare create irony out of Puck's summation of human behavior? How does a hobgoblin's mischief enhance suspense, atmosphere, conflict, plot resolution, and the theme of human weakness?

22. What attitudes do the characters display toward fatigue, confusion, rest, sleep, dreams, and nightmares? Which characters seem most distressed by danger, threats to virginity and reputation, and terrible visions? Why do Theseus and Hippolyta believe the wanderers' stories of chaotic events on the previous night?

23. Define comic relief with examples from Bottom's muddling of sense images. Why does Shakespeare choose confusion of seeing, hearing, tasting, and feeling as the basis of word play?

24. Justify the elopement of Hermia and Lysander. Why does Shakespeare create sympathy for Hermia, the childless widow, and her beloved nephew? Why does Egeus take no part in the last act?

25. How does Shakespeare contrast male and female values? Consider these instances:

    - Egeus's demand for his daughter's obedience
    - Oberon's intent to add the Indian boy to his forest patrol
    - the Indian priestess's enjoyment of seaside conversation
    - Bottom's insistence on clean, well-fitting masks and pumps, and on sweet breath
    - Hippolyta's despair at Hermia's choices of marriage to a man she doesn't love, death, or immurement in a convent
    - Titania's sympathy for peasant farmers and herders and the pain of arthritis
    - Hermia's love of a childhood friend
    - Demetrius's willingness to fight a duel over possession of Helena
    - Thisby's suicide at the sight of her dead lover
    - Hippolyta's dismay at the silly post-wedding performance
    - Hermia's refusal to sleep beside Lysander
    - Theseus's pride in Spartan hunting hounds
    - Philostrate's attempt to please his master

26. How does Shakespeare use rhymed couplets to round out significant speeches, for example:

    *Come our lovely lady nigh.*
    *So good night, with lullaby.*
    *And these things do best please me*
    *That befall prepost'rously.*
    *Jack shall have Jill;*
    *Naught shall go ill.*
    *Give me your hands, if we be friends,*
    *And Robin shall restore amends.*

27. What does Shakespeare imply about the fragility of human happiness? Why does he permeate a marriage play with references to the following?

- carnivorous animals
- dueling
- floods
- execution of a female
- ruined harvests
- hunting
- suicide
- a black fog
- worms and insects
- adultery
- hanging
- rape in the wild

- death in childbirth
- nightmares
- arthritis
- crows eating dead cattle
- a snake devouring a human heart
- deformed and birthmarked children
- kidnap of a woman in battle
- a bloody cloak
- sweethearts parted by a wall
- a ruined reputation

28. How does the last scene illustrate the value of three marriages to a well-ordered Athenian society? How does Shakespeare create irony out of the blessing issued by Puck, the trickster and mischief-maker?

29. Summarize the importance of midsummer and phases of the moon to the action. Why does the moon symbolize the following?

- chastity
- human fecundity
- transformation

- nature's control of human life and prosperity
- seasonal rhythms

30. Why does the self-important weaver Nick Bottom deserve the respect and concern of his fellow laborers? What does his name suggest about a core truth underlying human behaviors?

31. Why does Shakespeare contrast the older male lovers—Theseus and Oberon—with younger men, such as Lysander, Demetrius, and Pyramus? How does power corrupt the courtship of the Duke with Hippolyta and of the King of the Fairies with Titania?

32. What does the convention of dueling over a woman suggest about classical attitudes toward the bride? In what way does Theseus both follow and violate the convention of bride capture in combat? Why does Shakespeare strip Hippolyta of her belligerence as queen of the Amazons?

33. How does Shakespeare use the following standard human relationships in *A Midsummer Night's Dream?*

- girlhood friends
- vot'ress and queen
- father and daughter
- courting sweethearts
- parted lovers
- a duke and the laboring class
- ruler and noble subjects
- master and servant
- childless widow and foster son
- dueling rivals
- beardless boy and older man

34. How does Shakespeare use lowly people in a drama that also features a duke, Amazon queen, and king and queen of fairy land? How do cast members like the apprentice bellows mender, guardian sprite, vot'ress, weaver, master of revels, furniture maker, tin repairer, elves, carpenter, and servant boy contribute to the action? How does magic help Puck transcend social caste and the master/servant relationship with Oberon?

35. Describe the extreme emotions of the court masque. How did Shakespeare turn Oberon's vengeance into a source of confusion, alienation, misgivings, and violence?

36. Why did Elizabethan audiences like plays about troubled courtships, meddling, mischief, revenge, male-dominated matrimony, magic, holidays, mercy, generosity, and happy endings? What current performances echo those themes?

37. Write an extended definition of compromise using the following situations as examples:

- possession of an exotic servant boy
- a father's punishment of a disobedient daughter
- a duke's choice of nuptial entertainment for his court
- young rivals dueling over a pretty girlfriend
- a servant's attempt to keep his masters from quarreling
- appropriate behavior between unmarried people

38. Justify Shakespeare's use of mythic hero and heroine, a magic purple pansy blossom and chaste plant, Cupid's arrow, astrology, May Day, Valentine's Day, and fairies in a play about human love.

39. Characterize the role of the trickster by describing Puck's enthusiasm for mix-ups and ventriloquism. How does the name "Puck" contrast with "Robin Goodfellow"? Why does he occupy the middle ground between malice and blessing? How does his behavior illustrate the Asian concept of yin and yang?

40. Analyze the conclusion of the marriage masque. What does Shakespeare imply about procreation as the purpose of male-female wooing and union? Why was the topic a touchy subject for Queen Elizabeth and her advisers?